The Skeleton Coast

Praise for Mardi McConnochie's
The Flooded Earth

"McCONNOCHIE COVERS serious topics prevalent today through the journeys of four kids who provide touches of innocence in this gritty world....A bright adventure that touches upon a range of intense themes, from climate change to the refugee crisis."

— *Booklist*

"McCONNOCHIE DOES A FINE JOB of world-building, creating vivid images of abandoned waterfront communities and also developing the technical and governing structures that shape that world. The plot-driven adventure is deepened by interactions and revelations that shape the characters as they make their way across the ocean."

— *The Horn Book*

"[T]HIS ADVENTURE NOVEL is a strong series opener with a unique and timely concept. The fast-paced story will keep readers engaged, and solid world building will draw readers into this fascinating cli-fi (climate fiction) tale. A timely addition to most middle grade collections."

— *School Library Journal*

"AS IS TYPICAL of the cli-fi genre, McConnochie explores current-world issues within her adventure. Climate refugees and strict immigration laws have created a permanent underclass and a human trafficking problem, which privileged Essie begins to understand when the adventurers are joined by a starving former slave boy....Despite the post-disaster setting, an exciting and old-fashioned sailboat quest with pirates, secret codes, storms, and cannibals."

—*Kirkus Reviews*

"MARDI McCONNOCHIE'S middle grade, cli-fi dystopia is a wild adventure across a wildly different Earth....The magnificent capabilities of the book's determined young leads emerge as *The Flooded Earth*'s dominant force. Readers of this first in the series will be eager to learn where the team's sailboat takes them next..."

—*Foreword Reviews*

"QUESTIONS OF valuing human life, responsibly caring for the environment, proactively responding to natural disasters, and thoughtfully considering governmental authority could emerge as a result of reading this book...These advanced themes makes the story richer...In a racially charged society, focusing character development on relationships, rather than physical attributes, is mentally refreshing....**Recommended**."

—*School Library Connection*

Praise for Mardi McConnochie's
The Castle in the Sea

"AS IN THE FIRST BOOK, this sequel offers commentary on the refugee crisis, often using humor to alleviate the tense material, but McConnochie also delivers higher stakes, daring escapes, wild storms, and pirate battles in a second adventure sure to please young thrill-seekers."

—*Booklist*

"READERS WILL BE ENGROSSED in this action-packed adventure story and will eagerly await the next installment."

—*School Library Journal*

"THIS EQUALLY FAST-PACED, action-driven sequel to *The Flooded Earth*...begins to explore the scientific and ethical challenges of climate-altering technology, leaving plenty of questions to be resolved in the next volume."

—*The Horn Book Magazine*

"A POST-APOCALYPTIC DISASTER STORY with the cozy feel of *Swallows and Amazons*."

—*Kirkus Reviews*

**Publishers Weekly Noteworthy Novel
Sequels selection**

The Skeleton

Coast

Mardi McConnochie

pajamapress

First published in Canada and the United States in 2019

www.pajamapress.ca   info@pajamapress.ca

 Canada Council Conseil des arts
for the Arts du Canada    ONTARIO ARTS COUNCIL
CONSEIL DES ARTS DE L'ONTARIO
an Ontario government agency
un organisme du gouvernement de l'Ontario    Canada

The publisher gratefully acknowledges the support of the Canada Council for the Arts and
the Ontario Arts Council for its publishing program. We acknowledge the financial support
of the Government of Canada through the Canada Book Fund (CBF) for our publishing
activities.

Library and Archives Canada Cataloguing in Publication

Title: The Skeleton Coast / Mardi McConnochie.

Names: McConnochie, Mardi, 1971- author.

Description: Series statement: The flooded Earth ; 3 | "Originally published by Allen &
Unwin:

Crow's Nest, New South Wales, Australia, 2017."--Title page verso.

Identifiers: Canadiana 20190086637 | ISBN 9781772780994 (hardcover)

Classification: LCC PZ7.M4784133 S54 2019 | DDC j823/.92—dc23

Publisher Cataloging-in-Publication Data (U.S.)

Names: McConnochie, Mardi, 1971-, author.

Title: The Skeleton Coast / Mardi McConnochie.

Description: Toronto, Ontario Canada : Pajama Press, 2019. | Originally published by Allen
& Unwin, Australia, 2017 as The Skeleton Coast: Quest of the Sunfish 3 | Series: The
Flooded Earth Trilogy. | Summary: "In a future where a botched scientific experiment has
flooded the planet, twins Will and Annalie finally set a course to intercept their father.
He is protecting research about the flood's origins that the corrupt Admiralty is bent on
turning to their own sinister purposes"— Provided by publisher.

Identifiers: ISBN 978-1-77278-099-4 (hardcover)

Subjects: LCSH: Twins – Juvenile fiction. | Floods – Juvenile fiction. | – Juvenile fiction.
| Missing persons – Juvenile fiction. | BISAC: JUVENILE FICTION / Science fiction.
| JUVENILE FICTION / Action & Adventure / Pirates. | JUVENILE FICTION /
Dystopian.

Classification: LCC PZ7.M336Ske |DDC [F] – dc23

Cover design by Rebecca Buchanan
Text design based on original by Midland Typesetters, Australia

Manufactured by Friesens
Printed in Canada

Pajama Press Inc.
181 Carlaw Ave., Suite 251, Toronto, Ontario Canada, M4M 2S1

Distributed in Canada by UTP Distribution
5201 Dufferin Street Toronto, Ontario Canada, M3H 5T8

Distributed in the U.S. by Ingram Publisher Services
1 Ingram Blvd. La Vergne, TN 37086, USA

For Annabelle and Lila
and for James, who makes everything possible

Pirates!

The gray light of dawn crept through the sky. The sun was yet to make its first appearance, but the crew of the *Sunfish* were already up and ready to weigh anchor.

The previous night, they had come agonizingly close to catching up with Spinner; then Commander Avery Beckett's men intervened with fiery results, and Spinner fled once again, heading for the remote island nation of Sundia, leaving Will, Annalie, Essie, Pod, and Graham behind.

Will had been all for setting sail for Sundia straight away, even though it was after midnight. The others had had to remind him that the *Sunfish* was still on the edge of a debris field and that they couldn't risk crashing into any more underwater obstacles in the dark.

But now the sun was almost up. They could see what lay ahead of them. It was time to go.

They sailed out into the ocean, leaving the coast of Brundisi behind them. Just as the sun made its first peep over the horizon, Graham let out a warning squawk.

"Uh oh." Pod grabbed the binoculars.

"What can you see?" asked Will.

"Pirates," Pod said. "Three of them."

"That's not so bad—"

"Three *boats*."

Will looked at Pod in dismay, then called to the others. "Annalie! Essie! We've got trouble!"

"Head straight out to sea," Pod said. "They're going to try and drive us back into the debris field, but don't let them."

"I won't," Will said with grim determination.

The girls came hurrying up from below and put up more sail.

"Do you think these are the same guys as before?" Annalie asked Pod.

"Them or their friends," Pod said. "Either way, they're bad news. At least this time we've got guns."

"Wait—what?" said Annalie.

"We weren't sure what to do with them," Essie explained. "So we kept them."

Annalie stared at Pod and Essie. "And you're only just mentioning this now?"

"Who cares?" Will shouted. "We can finally put up a decent fight!"

"I told you," Pod said to Essie.

"We don't even know how to use them!" Annalie said.

"That's what I said you'd say," Essie said.

"*I* know how to use them," Pod said, just as Will said, "How hard can it be? Go get them!"

Pod rushed off.

"I don't like this," Annalie said. "What if shooting at them just escalates things?"

"There are three boats full of them," Will said. "Without guns, we don't stand a chance."

"They're getting closer," Essie warned.

The three fast-moving speedboats sent up three plumes of white water as three sets of pirates came weaving through the debris field toward them. Fast, light, maneuverable, deadly, they could easily outpace the sailboat.

"Maybe we should call for help," Essie suggested, holding up her shell.

"Who are we going to call?" Will asked.

"There's an emergency channel," Annalie said, glaring at Will. "It's worth a try."

Essie tried, but then looked disappointed. "Oh. No signal."

"Story of our lives," Will said. "Are they gaining on us?"

"Yep," Pod said, returning with the two big guns. "Who wants one?"

"Me!" Will said.

"Who's going to steer the boat?" objected Annalie.

"You," Will said, reaching for a gun. "Now, how does this work?"

Annalie took the wheel as the two boys studied the guns.

"It's been a while since I ..." Pod murmured, turning the weapon over. He accidentally released the clip, which fell onto the deck.

"Outlaw Pod," Graham taunted. Pod ignored him.

"Is that the ammo? How much have we got?" Will asked.

"Some," Pod said, reaching for the other gun and checking that clip too. "Not a huge amount."

"Did you get any more clips?"

"No."

"Why not?"

"If I'd seen any, I would have taken them," Pod retorted huffily. "Maybe they didn't bring any with them on the boat. And I didn't really want to go through their pockets in case they woke up again."

"Okay, fine," Will said. "So how exactly do I use this?"

The three boats were in open water now, fanning out to surround them on all sides and try to drive them back into the debris, where the pirates would have the advantage.

"What's the play?" Annalie called to Will, as Pod hurried below with one of the guns to lie in wait in the saloon.

"Keep sailing and don't stop," Will said, concealing himself under a tarp on deck.

Annalie did her best, running with the wind in the forlorn hope of evading their pursuers, but the three pirate boats could not be outrun. Soon the *Sunfish* was surrounded, and the three little boats were cutting across their bow while the men in them shouted and brandished their weapons.

"I think they want us to stop," Annalie said.

"Don't," Will said from under the tarp. "Why make it easier for them?"

They surged on; there was a good wind behind them, and the sails pulled them eagerly forwards.

4

But it was not enough; the pirates kept zigzagging across, coming so close that Annalie was convinced they would collide with the *Sunfish*. The pirate boats had metal hulls; a collision would almost certainly be worse for the *Sunfish* than for the pirates. One of them skimmed so close to their bow that Annalie could almost hear them scraping.

"They're going to take us down!" she cried.

"They're just trying to scare you," Will said. "Don't let them!" He grinned at her. "If they want my boat, they're going to have to work for it!"

"If they want *whose* boat?" Annalie retorted.

Closer they came, closer and closer, and the guns waved and the men shouted, but still no shots had been fired, and still the *Sunfish* sailed on, further and further from the coast of Brundisi, and Annalie began to hope that perhaps they might be able to keep running long enough for the pirates to get sick of it and give up. But of course, pirates didn't give up.

"Annalie!" Essie shrieked. "Look!"

One of the little boats had swung close enough to let a pirate leap from the moving dinghy directly onto the ladder at the back.

He was on deck in a flash, and his rifle—just like the one Will held—was pointed directly at Annalie. He shouted something, which was probably "Surrender, or I'll shoot." Annalie, watching him cautiously, slowly took her hands off the wheel and put them in the air.

The pirate, who was short and wiry and had a red bandana tied around his head, grinned at her and began advancing, step by step, toward the wheel. He shouted something to the other pirates, who were circling in closer now.

Essie stood there in an agony of fear, waiting for Will to make his move. If he was going to take on the pirate, shouldn't he do it now?

But Will held on, waiting for his moment. He knew he could only surprise them once. If he broke cover too soon, it could all be over very quickly.

Red Bandana shouted something over his shoulder. His dinghy came circling in toward the *Sunfish* again, and soon the pirates were tying up so more of them could come aboard. Red Bandana turned back to Annalie and Essie and shouted something else, pointing at the sails.

"I think he wants us to take the sails down," Essie said.

"Yep," Annalie said.

"Should we?"

"He's got the gun."

Unwillingly, Annalie and Essie set to work on the sails. They made slow progress—working at gunpoint was terrifying, and Essie's hands were shaking so much she could hardly control them.

A second pirate came aboard, then a third. The second wore a jaunty blue hat, and he said in accented Duxish, "How many you?"

"It's just us," Annalie said.

Blue Hat and Red Bandana shared an evil grin. "Nice boat," Blue Hat said. "I think I keep."

He turned to the third, bearded pirate and spoke to him in his own language. Beardy came toward the girls, and for a moment they both froze, afraid of what he might be about to do, but he simply pushed them out of the way and began to take down the sails. He had arms like knotted ropes; in his hands, the sails would be down in minutes.

"What are you going to do with us?" Annalie asked, trying to keep the other pirates distracted.

"You got money?"

"Yes," Essie said quickly. "I mean, my father does."

"Where he?" asked Blue Hat. "He here? Brundisi?"

"Back in Dux," Essie said. "He's very rich."

"He better be," Blue Hat said.

Blue Hat turned and gave Red Bandana an order. Red Bandana grabbed Annalie and began to tie her hands behind her back. Annalie struggled, but the pirate was too strong for her. In no time, she was tied up tight, and Red Bandana was lashing her to the mast, where there could be no chance of her making any trouble. Then he went back for Essie.

Will, what's taking you so long? Annalie wondered as Red Bandana began tying Essie up too.

Will was still lying concealed, his gun at the ready, trying to decide what to do. There had been three pirates on the first dinghy. From what he could glimpse of the other two dinghies, which were now cruising beside the *Sunfish*, there were no more than three in either of those—that meant nine pirates in all. He could feel the *Sunfish* slowing as the sails came down one by one. Nine pirates wasn't so many, right? He and Pod could handle nine of them between them, couldn't they? Especially since they still had the element of surprise.

7

An engine roared nearby, and he realized the second dinghy was coming alongside. Three more pirates came aboard and conferred with the first group. They looked at the girls tied to the mast and discussed them for a while. Then Blue Hat turned to Annalie and said, "Just you two on boat, right?"

"That's right," Annalie said.

"We don't like surprises," Blue Hat warned.

Two of the second group of pirates went to the door that led below. They were going down to check the saloon.

Will clutched his gun a little tighter, feeling a surge of adrenaline. As soon as they discovered Pod, it would all be on.

Pod stood behind the door to the cabin he shared with Will, the stolen gun in his hands, waiting. It felt rather strange to be in this position. The last time he'd held a gun, he had been a pirate, and part of a boarding party just like this one.

Before he joined the crew of the *Sunfish*, Pod had been a reluctant pirate—it had seemed a better fate than being stuck in a dark, stinking slaver's ship, and at least on a pirate ship he had a job, and the possibility of a future. He had not wanted to be in the business of hunting down boats, stripping them of everything of value, and then ransoming their crews. But you couldn't say "Actually, I'd rather not" to your pirate master, so during the year he'd spent with the pirates, he'd picked up a gun and learned how to use it, climbed on boats just like this one, and made himself useful working through holds and cabins and lockers searching for valuables. He remembered exactly how terrifying it was, creeping around some boat you didn't know, never knowing who or what might be lying in wait. Once or twice he'd even had to defend himself against grown-ups twice his size. Fortunately, he'd lived to tell the tale, and only had one knife scar to show for it. But he'd never actually fired a gun in anger. He'd shot at things for practice, of course. His master had insisted on it, making him shoot at targets over and over again until he could hit a mark without messing it up. But an actual person? Never.

When he had joined the *Sunfish*, he'd hoped all that was behind him. Yet now here he was, lying in wait, with a gun in his hand.

He could hear them all moving around above, shouting to one another. He'd heard the second group of pirates come aboard—more feet, more shouting. Any moment now, he knew, they would come downstairs. And then he'd have to decide what to do.

"Pod ready?" Graham croaked. He was perched on the bed, watching him. "Kill pirates?"

"I'd rather not have to kill anyone," Pod said. "You stay out of the way, okay? I don't want you getting caught in the crossfire."

"Graham fast."

"Yeah, but bullets are faster."

Something creaked.

"This is it," Pod whispered.

9

He peered through the crack between the cabin door and the wall.

A pirate in a yellow shirt was coming down the stairs and into the saloon, a second pirate in green right behind him. They crept down cautiously, guns at the ready, sizing up the place. Pod studied them; they were armed with hunting knives as well as guns, and they were barefoot. Yellow Shirt pointed to the cabin door opposite; Green Shirt quickly slammed it open and looked in. Empty. Green Shirt threw open the door to the heads next. Empty. Then he turned to the last cabin door. Pod's door.

Pod got his gun into position; his finger on the trigger. He took a step back from the door, knowing they would smash it open.

Slam! The door opened.

Bang! Pod fired.

Bullets blasted in a ghastly spray, and the pirates crashed to the floor. Pod jumped over them and ran into the saloon, not really wanting to know what his gun had done to them. He could already hear shouting and screaming from above. He took a big glass coffee pot from a locker in the galley and smashed it on the floor so that glass went everywhere. Then he turned back to the pirates. Green Shirt wasn't moving at all. Yellow Shirt was moaning and writhing. Pod looked around for something to tie them up with, but couldn't find anything easily to hand, and he was afraid that more pirates could come down the stairs at any moment. Giving up on that idea—for now, at least—he fought grimly with Yellow Shirt for his weapons.

Yellow Shirt fought hard, but he was bleeding a lot and he seemed confused. Pod got hold of both guns and both knives, then pushed both pirates into the cabin, slammed the door, and locked it from the outside. The cabin doors had been designed to be sealable in the case of a hull breach, so he knew they were pretty securely locked away, at least until someone came along to let them out.

He took the confiscated guns and knives and hid them. Then he went behind the cabin door again to wait for the next wave.

"You said no more people!" Blue Hat shouted, running at Annalie. Red Bandana had his gun pointed right up in her face. "How many? *How many?*"

Annalie scrinched away from the gun, still tied to the mast, and at last Will saw his moment.

"Wouldn't you like to know?" he shouted, jumping to his feet. He pointed his gun at Red Bandana and pulled the trigger. The gun's powerful action caught him by surprise and it jerked in his hands, spraying bullets haphazardly across the deck. Red Bandana spun and fell, clipped by a bullet, but Blue Hat and Beardy were unharmed.

Beardy pointed his own gun at Will.

"Drop the gun, kid!" Blue Hat said, but Will wasn't done yet. He took a better grip on his weapon and tried again—but this time, nothing happened. He squeezed the trigger again. Still nothing happened. The gun had jammed.

Panic flooded through Will in a black tide, and Blue Hat grinned. "Tie him up, too," he ordered.

11

Beardy came toward Will, who backed all the way up to the railing. Then an idea struck him—and he flipped himself over the railing and into the water.

Blue Hat shouted in fury and ran to the railing to see where Will had gone.

"What is he doing?" Essie whispered to Annalie.

"I have no idea," Annalie said.

An argument broke out between Blue Hat and the last of the second wave of pirates, who was wearing a faded football shirt. They seemed to be shouting about whether they should be chasing after Will or going down to the saloon to find out what had happened. Blue Hat, it appeared, wanted to go after Will, but Football Shirt was more interested in finding out whether his men were okay. After more shouting and arguing than seemed entirely necessary, Football Shirt took Beardy and went below, while Blue Hat went back to looking for Will.

Pod waited, his gun at the ready.

There. Now. Feet descending—two more of them.

He let them both get down into the saloon. Shattered glass lay everywhere. The first one, a bearded man, stepped on some and swore. The second man spotted the blood on the floor, and his eyes widened.

Pod fired.

Will came up from underwater cautiously. He'd been hiding under the boat, holding his breath for as long as he could. Now he swam to one of the empty pirate dinghies and quickly swung himself into it. He'd hoped there might be more weapons aboard, but there weren't. Improvising, he cast off, started the engine, and drove away from the *Sunfish* at top speed.

Behind him, he could hear Blue Hat hollering. The third dinghy swung out from behind the *Sunfish* and gave chase, just as he'd hoped they would. Gunfire rattled, but nothing hit him. He hoped they were just trying to scare him.

He steered around in a great arc until he could see the distant shape of Brundisi in front of him and made straight for it.

Blue Hat stood on the deck for a moment, watching the third dinghy race off after Will. Then he turned and looked back toward the saloon.

Four men had gone down there. None, yet, had come back up. Red Bandana still lay on the deck where he'd fallen.

Annalie and Essie watched Blue Hat as he sized up the situation. For a moment, Annalie had the dizzying feeling that they might actually be able to win this. Could they really succeed against armed pirates?

Blue Hat took a knife from his belt and came toward them, an angry snarl on his face. Essie was his target, and she couldn't help a squeak of terror as he brandished the knife at her. But no—he wasn't going to cut her. The knife sliced through the rope holding her to the mast, leaving her hands still bound behind her. He grabbed her around the neck, held the knife to her throat, and said, "If your friend shoots, you die. You tell! Understand?"

Essie stared at him, too frightened to process what he was saying. "You tell your friend!" he repeated angrily. "Tell him! Understand?"

"Okay, I get it," Essie said.

Blue Hat marched her to the stairs, holding her in front of him, his knife pressed to her throat. He stopped her at the top of the stairs and said again, "You tell!"

"We're coming down," Essie called, her voice wobbling. "Don't shoot me! Okay?"

And then the two of them began to descend step by step into the saloon.

Will glanced over his shoulder. The third dinghy was still on his tail, and the *Sunfish* was now far behind them. He slalomed on, heading to shore. The water became shallower. Underwater obstacles turned into green, slimy stubs. Broken roofs, pieces of wall, pylons and metal and concrete. He could not now skim over them; he was having to zig and zag, twist and turn, picking a path through the debris. Open sea was becoming a watery streetscape, the rubble turning back into wet-footed buildings. And as the buildings emerged from the water, people began to appear. Brundisi before the Flood had been one of the most densely populated countries in the world, and it still teemed with people. Even here at the water's edge, where high tides regularly inundated old houses, people lived and worked, washed and cooked and shopped. Some of these people looked up or shouted and shook their fists at Will as he roared past, the wake of his engine setting up a mighty chop that slapped against the houses.

On he flew, and the pirates flew along behind him. He had hoped that, once he was among these twisty streets, it would be easy to give the pirates the slip, but now he realized that they were actually gaining on him. They knew these waterways; they lived them, traveled them, every single day.

Too late to think about that now. All he could do was race on.

He sped up.

It was getting dangerous now as he zoomed around blind corners and cut across slower moving traffic. He had not hit anything—he trusted he would not hit anything—but he had near miss after near miss—a corner that hid a protruding wall! A pole sticking out of the water! A slow-moving ferry! A woman with washing! A family of water birds!—until he was breathless and desperate to get out of there. A few minutes had gone by since he had seen or heard the third dinghy, and he began to wonder if he'd managed to shed them after all and whether it was time to head back out to sea again, when something came roaring around a curve. To his horror, he saw the third dinghy appear directly in front of him.

The pirates on board grinned and pointed their guns at him.

Will swung around in a circle and tried to lose himself once more in the maze of streets. They hadn't fired at him; Will hoped that when the streets were teeming with their own people, they wouldn't dare shoot, since they'd be just as likely to hit six other people at the same time. But he didn't know just how bad these guys actually were. Maybe they didn't care who they hit if it meant they got what they wanted. He roared on, now with very little idea even which direction he was traveling in. The buildings around him were high enough that it was hard to tell whether he was heading deeper inland or back out to sea. He could hear the roar of the third dinghy behind him. They had him, and they would not let him go.

Will began to think that this had not been his best idea ever.

Gulping down his fear, he kept on. He'd found himself on a busier waterway, and a few moments later, he understood why. The street he was on ended and suddenly he was out in a wide-open space: it was more like a river than a channel. In fact, it was the harbor he'd been through yesterday with Annalie.

And there, riding at anchor slap-bang in the middle of it, was the same Admiralty ship they'd tried so hard to avoid.

Will had never been so happy to see the Admiralty in all his life. He steered toward it and did a pass right along its side, hoping to get the Admiralty crew's attention, knowing that the pirate dinghy was

16

coming up behind him. Then he began racing down the channel as fast as he could go, heading for open sea once more.

The pirate dinghy burst out into the channel behind him. Will glanced back, hoping the presence of the Admiralty ship would deter them from chasing him any further. It didn't. The three pirates in the dinghy were so intent on him they didn't seem to care that there was an Admiralty ship right there. They turned their engine up full throttle and came after him, guns at the ready.

Will's heart sank. He'd been sure the presence of the Admiralty would frighten the pirates off. It had certainly frightened *him* when he saw them yesterday. But nothing seemed to scare these guys. He would simply have to try and outrun them.

Now it was just a speed game—who could go faster? The two boats were identical, and both drivers were equally determined. Will's dinghy, with only one person in it, sat a little higher in the water. Will headed for open sea once more.

Essie took one trembling step down the stairs, then another. The saloon smelled horribly of gunpowder and blood. She knew Pod must be down here somewhere, but she couldn't see him. Glass was strewn over the floor. Blue Hat held her tightly, the knife prickling against her throat.

"Pod?" she said. "Please don't shoot."

"You try anything," Blue Hat called, his voice very loud in her ear, "I cut your friend. I'll do it!"

For a long moment there was silence, and then they heard a muffled banging coming from the cabin. Blue Hat called something in his own language, and some other voices responded from the other side of the door.

"You got four of my people," Blue Hat warned. "But I got two of yours. Better come out now, or bad things gonna happen."

Still there was silence. Blue Hat kept swiveling cautiously, not sure where Pod was hiding in the narrow space, knowing he had to be close.

"I count to three," he said, "then I cut. One ... Two ..."

There was a sudden eruption of feathers and squawking from behind the cabin door. Graham flew at Blue Hat, screeching and furious, his ferocious claws extended. Blue Hat momentarily relaxed his grip on Essie as he fended off Graham. She twisted away from him and stumbled into the saloon, glass crunching underfoot, only to see Blue Hat swing viciously at Graham with his knife. Suddenly there was blood on feathers, Graham was tumbling to the floor, and Pod erupted from the cabin door with a great cry of "No!" Blue Hat lunged for Pod, grabbing the other end of the gun he held and wrenching it from his grasp. The pirate swung it around and covered both Pod and Essie with the gun, and suddenly it was all over.

Blue Hat grinned. "Kids shouldn't play with guns," he said.

He took a step over to the other cabin and unlocked it, setting free the other four pirates, who were bloodied and wounded but alive.

"Now," he said to Essie. "What you say about a rich daddy?"

Up on deck, Annalie waited tensely. There had been no more shots fired, but she could hear voices. What was going on down there?

Suddenly, there was movement beside her. Red Bandana, who'd been felled by Will's first and only spray of bullets, was clambering to his feet. Blood seeped from a wound on his head, but it didn't seem to be troubling him. His eyes glinted with greedy malice as he looked around the boat, trying to understand what had happened.

His gaze swiveled back to Annalie, now alone at the mast. He looked thoughtfully at the door that led down to the saloon, then came to a swift decision. He walked toward her, pulling his knife from his belt.

Will could see the *Sunfish* now, dead ahead. The sails were down and she was adrift. He peered up ahead, trying to see what was going on. There was no one on deck, and the first pirate dinghy was missing. Was that a good sign? A bad sign? Had Pod somehow, miraculously, managed to retake the boat from the pirates by shooting his way out of the saloon?

Or was he too late, and the pirates had already taken the others prisoner?

He zoomed up to the *Sunfish* and slowed to a stop, his mind already racing ahead. At least some of the pirates could still be aboard, so what could he use as a weapon? His speargun, which had proven itself before as a weapon against the Admiralty, was unfortunately secured in a locker down below. The slingshot was also somewhere below, probably in the girls' cabin. Essie had used it very effectively on the pirates who'd come after them yesterday, but he wondered if the same trick would work twice, even if he could get to it.

He tied up the dinghy and crept up the ladder, sticking his head up for a cautious look around. Nope—definitely no one on deck. He went over to the doorway that led to the saloon, hoping he might be able to hear what was going on down there.

Voices. Not Pod or Essie or Annalie's voices.

The pirates were still here, then.

Moving as quietly as he could, he crept across the deck to an equipment locker, pulled out some heavy metal weights, quickly tied them to the end of a rope, and then moved into position.

The roar of the third dinghy grew louder and then the engine stopped. Will got a firm grip on the rope. The first pirate head came up—and Will let fly with the rope. The heavy weight smashed into the pirate's arm and he yelled in pain and fury, dropping back out of sight. A second pirate head appeared, this time with a gun. Will swung again, but missed; the second pirate recovered and trained the gun on him. The pirate shouted something; answering shouts came from below, and a third pirate came climbing up the

20

ladder. He grabbed Will securely as Blue Hat came up from below decks.

"Little thief back?" He smiled unpleasantly. "You have rich daddy, too? Or do we just kill you now?"

He repeated what he'd said in his own language and the other pirates laughed. The pirate with the gun came closer, closer—

And then Will heard something.

Another high-powered motor. At first he thought it must be the first dinghy returning to the *Sunfish*. But then he noticed the looks of dismay on the pirates' faces. Whoever was coming, it was not their friends.

He turned and saw two large inflatable boats filled with Admiralty marines zipping toward them. They were exactly the same kind of inflatables that the Admiralty had sent after the *Sunfish* when they were chasing them across the Emperor Reef, but this time it appeared—or at least Will hoped—the marines might be on their side.

The pirates from the third dinghy abandoned the job immediately, practically shoving each other out of the way to get back to their dinghy and escape. They went zooming off back toward Brundisi, and one of the two Admiralty inflatables peeled smoothly off and went after them, leaving the other one to come gliding up to the *Sunfish*.

Will ran to the side, his hands in the air, and shouted to the marines. "Quick! Please! Help us! These pirates attacked us!"

Behind him, he could hear some of the pirates talking to each other in quick, angry tones.

A marine was giving orders through a loudspeaker. "Unknown vessel, stand down immediately! Lower your weapons and put your hands in the air!" The same message was then repeated in Brundisan.

Will still had his hands in the air. He turned anxiously to see what the pirates were doing, hoping this wasn't about to turn into a shoot-out, and saw them muttering and gesticulating angrily. None of them had put down their weapons.

"Stand down now!" the marine ordered.

Blue Hat was arguing with Football Shirt. Suddenly Green Shirt swung his gun and sprayed the Admiralty inflatable. He didn't hit anything, but at once all the marines had their own weapons trained on the pirates. There was a single, sharp crack, and Green Shirt crashed to the deck with a yelp, his gun skittering across the deck.

"Place your weapons on the deck and put your hands in the air now!" the marine said again.

This time, there was no further argument. The pirates slowly and unwillingly dropped their weapons one by one and put their hands in the air.

The marines swarmed aboard, and while they were busy handcuffing the pirates, their commanding officer spoke to Will. "What happened here?" she asked. "Was anybody hurt? Are you in need of medical assistance?"

"I don't know," Will said, starting to feel afraid that he still hadn't seen any sign of the others. "I left the boat to try and lead the pirates away. I only just got back. My friends and my sister—I left them behind— they could be down below—"

He darted for the stairs to the saloon, but the marine commander stopped him. "Wait. We'll make sure it's secure."

Will waited, filled with anxiety, as two marines went below, weapons at the ready. They weren't gone for long before they quickly reappeared with Pod and Essie.

"Are these your friends?" the marine commander asked.

"Yes, but—where's Annalie?" Will asked.

"She was up here," Essie said, starting to look frightened. "When that guy made me go downstairs, he left her here on the deck. Didn't you see her?"

Will stared at her for a moment, unable to make sense of this. Then he realized what must have happened. Either Annalie had somehow managed to get free, taken the missing dinghy and escaped, or someone had kidnapped her.

"Is something wrong?" the marine commander asked. "Is someone missing?"

"Actually, no," Will said. "I know where she is. We're all fine here."

Essie and Pod looked at him in astonishment.

"Thank you so much for rescuing us, though," Will said, trying his hardest to sound sincere and trustworthy. "We were lucky you came along when you did. They just about had us. So are we going to be all right to go soon?"

"Go? We can't authorize you to leave yet. We'll need you to come back to our vessel and make a report."

"Oh," Will said. "Sure. Very happy to make a report. Thing is, we're just waiting for our other crew member to come back. She's off getting supplies now, but she won't be gone for long. Would we be able to come and make our report as soon as she's back?"

The marine commander looked at him through narrowed eyes. "We can stay and escort you back to our vessel. We don't mind waiting."

"No, we don't need an escort. Just give us an hour or so. Two, max. And then we'll fill out a complete report. We definitely want you to throw the book at these guys."

"Right," the marine commander said. She obviously wanted to get back to processing the pirates, but she was still a little skeptical about what was going on here. "Are there any adults on board this vessel?"

"My sister, the one who's coming back. She's the adult," Will said.

The marine commander gave him one final look, then nodded. "Okay," she said, "but don't leave it too long. We're shipping out ourselves soon."

"Roger that," Will said. "And thanks again for saving us."

"Yes, thank you," Essie said.

Pod was mute.

The marine commander nodded, but said, "You know, you shouldn't be out here. These are dangerous waters."

"No kidding," Will said. The commander gave him a stern look. "I mean, yes, we know. We'll go as soon as we can."

The three of them waited in silence as the marines finished handcuffing the pirates and collecting all their weapons. Then the pirates were separated into two groups and taken off the *Sunfish*, some in the pirates' own dinghy, the rest on the Admiralty inflatable.

"I wish they'd let us keep that dinghy," Will sighed as the marines pulled away. Then he turned to the others. "Okay, now let's get out of here."

"Go where?"

"What are you talking about? What about Annalie?!"

Pod and Essie spoke over each other.

"Either she's escaped, or the pirates have her," Will said. "Either way, we can't stick around here and let the Admiralty work out who we really are. Right now, they think we're just stupid civilians. But that's the same boat that was here looking for Spinner—for all we know, Beckett himself could be aboard. As soon as those marines get back to their own vessel and make their report, someone might begin to figure it out. We've got to get away from here before they come back for us."

"But if Annalie really has been kidnapped, wouldn't the Admiralty have a better chance of finding her than we will?" Essie asked.

"Do you want us all to get arrested?" Will said.

"I want her not to be dead!" Essie shot back.

"We'll think of a way to get her back," Will said. "But we can't do anything if Beckett's got us locked up."

"What if she did escape?" Essie persisted. "How will she know how to find us?"

"Do you really think she escaped?" Will asked.

Essie shrugged unhappily. "She *might* have ..."

"More likely someone saw their chance, grabbed a hostage and ran," Pod said gloomily.

"Either way," Will said, "we can't hang around here any longer. I don't want either of them finding us again—pirates *or* Admiralty."

Pod nodded his agreement and so, reluctantly, did Essie.

"I'll get the sails up," Pod said. "Essie, you should go and check on Graham."

"Wait," Will said, "what happened to Graham?"

Graham

"Graham?" Essie called. "Are you okay?"

She crunched over the broken glass, looking around. There was no sign of him. "The pirates are gone now," she called, "and so are the Admiralty. We're safe. There's no one here but us."

She heard a caw from one of the cabins.

A cupboard door creaked open as she walked in. She hurried over; Graham had pushed it open with his beak but could manage no more. The pirate's knife had sliced into his wing, which was hanging at an odd angle, dark with blood.

"Oh, you poor thing!" she said, reaching for him, but Graham snapped at her. Essie quickly pulled her hand away. "Tell you what, I'll go and fetch the first aid kit and send Pod down," she said.

Pod came soon enough, and picked Graham up tenderly. "You've been in the wars," he murmured. "How's that wing? Does it hurt?"

"Course it hurts!" Graham rasped.

"Think you can fly?"

Graham shook his head no.

Pod looked at the wound and didn't like what

27

he saw. It was deep, and if it had cut through vital muscles or ligaments, Graham might never fly again. "Let's bandage this up, for starters," he said.

Pod, assisted by Essie, bandaged the wing, while Graham winced and swore at them. When he was done, Pod found him a biscuit. "You're a brave old bird," he said, "taking on that pirate. He was one scary guy."

"Graham not scared," Graham said. "Pod fight, Graham fight, too."

"Next time, pick on someone your own size," Pod said.

"Next time, pick fight with bird," Graham said, nibbling on his biscuit, his eyes drooping with fatigue.

"We'll let you get some rest," Pod said.

"He doesn't look too good," Essie said quietly as they left the cabin.

"I know," Pod said. "I wish we could find him a bird doctor."

"You mean a vet?" Essie said. "Where would we find one around here?"

Pod shrugged.

Will had set a course for the east, across the Sea of Brundisi, away from the pirates who'd attacked them and also, he hoped, away from the Admiralty ship. "Well?" he asked as Pod and Essie reappeared on deck. "How's he doing?"

"Knife wound," Pod said. "It's bad."

"Going-to-die bad?"

"Hopefully not," Pod said. "But possibly not-able-to-fly bad if we don't get him looked at."

"Looked at?" Will echoed. "Around here?" He gestured back toward the Brundisi shore. "I don't reckon there's a lot of neighborhood vets in Dio. Not a lot of cats and dogs needing their claws clipped."

"You asked," Pod said stubbornly. "I'm telling you."

"You do remember that's not our only problem, don't you?" Will said. "We still have to find Annalie."

"I thought you had a plan," Pod said.

"Of course I don't have a plan," Will said crossly. "I just knew we had to get out of the last mess before we work out how to get ourselves out of the next one!"

They all turned to look back at the vast, sprawling, hostile cityscape, veiled by a smoky haze. Annalie was in there somewhere, but so were the pirates, and so were the Admiralty.

"Maybe we can try and get in contact with Spinner's friend's people," Pod said. "They might know what to do—who to ask—"

"Vesh's place just got blown up by the Admiralty, remember?" Will said. "I saw it burn to the ground. Maybe Vesh had friends here, I assume he did, but I wouldn't have a clue how to get in touch with them now. We'll just have to think of some other way to find Annalie."

"Did she have her shell on her?" Pod asked.

"I'll check," Essie said, and ran down to the cabin to check. Bad news—she returned, holding it.

"We can't find her that way," Will said. "And she can't contact us either."

For a moment, they were all sunk in gloom. Then

Essie said, "Hang on, we don't have to work out how to find her. *They'll* contact *us*. They want a ransom, right? As soon as they start looking for money, she'll tell them to call us."

"Yeah, but then what?" said Pod.

"Well, then we just try and get her back," Essie said.

"How?" Will said.

"Maybe we just have to give them some money."

"We've got almost no money left," Will said. "Your dad's creditstream's been blocked, and they're monitoring his communications. If you go to him for money, they'll be able to track us."

"I know," Essie admitted, and frowned. "But there's got to be a way. Here's another problem, though." She held up her shell. "No signal. The kidnappers can't get in touch with us while we're out at sea."

"I'm not in a hurry to go back to Dio," Will said.

"Isn't there some safer bit up or down the coast somewhere?" Pod asked.

Will shrugged eloquently. "One bit's as dangerous as another if you don't know where you're going."

"What about Gantua?" Essie suggested. "There's signal, there are services, and they don't have any pirates. We can probably track down a vet for Graham, too."

Gantua was Brundisi's eastern neighbor, but the two countries had very little in common. Gantua and Brundisi spoke different languages and practiced different religions. A tall mountain range partially separated them; for centuries, they had invaded one

30

another as various dynasties waxed and waned. In the years leading up to the Flood, rain continued to fall on the Gantuan side of the mountains, but stopped on the Brundisan side. After the Flood, the Gantuans had eagerly joined forces with the Admiralty. Gantua, as a consequence, was still a functioning state, while Brundisi was a failed state.

"And no pirates there?" Pod asked.

"Nope, no pirates," Will said. He looked at the others. "So what do you think?"

"It feels kind of weird sailing off and leaving Annalie behind," Essie said.

"We're not leaving her, exactly," Will said. "We're putting ourselves in a position where we can actually do something to help her."

"We'll be a long way away if she needs us in a hurry," Pod said soberly. "But we need to get help for Graham. We can't fix him by ourselves."

"We'll go to Gantua, find a vet, and try to come up with a plan," Will said, trying to sound more confident than he felt. "We'll get her back. I know we can."

Kidnapped

Annalie did not normally get seasick. But she did not normally ride over bouncing waves, pressed into the bottom of a metal dinghy, with her hands tied behind her back and a bag over her head either. The longer the ride went on, the more nauseated she got, and the more bruised she felt from being slammed unpredictably against the bottom of the dinghy. Red Bandana had hidden her under a tarp and given her very stern instructions which she couldn't understand but which she guessed probably meant "Don't come out until I tell you." He kept his foot on her for good measure. She lay there, hot, bruised, gasping for breath, growing sicker and sicker. Just as she was beginning to think she could not bear it for another second, she heard the engine throttling back; the bouncing slowed to a gentle cruise, and then the dinghy slowed and stopped.

The tarp was thrown back, although the bag over her head stayed in place. She was pulled to her feet, the dinghy rocking wildly beneath her. More hands steadied and hauled her onto solid ground. She guessed she was standing on some sort of wooden boardwalk; yesterday, as she traveled through the waterlogged outskirts of Dio, she'd noticed rickety wooden walkways built above the high tide level, which meant that people could move between the upper storeys of these buildings, even though water lapped at their lower floors. She was pushed, stumbling, along the walkway and then into a maze-like interior with many twists and turns, layered with different smells: unfamiliar cooking, seawater, mildew. She heard a bolt being shot, and at last, the bag was taken from her head. She barely caught a glimpse of a dark nondescript corridor before Red Bandana pushed her through a door and slammed it shut again.

"Hey!" she cried. "Aren't you going to untie me?"

The only answer she got was the sound of the bolt being shot and padlocked again.

"Perhaps I can help you with that," a voice said.

Annalie turned and saw a young man with fair hair and a round face getting to his feet. She gasped in shock when she saw him, and not just because the side of his head and his jacket were spattered with dark, dried blood. He was also dressed in the uniform of a first year Admiralty officer.

"I'm Lieutenant Cherry," he said. "What's your name?"

Someone always pays

Annalie stared at him. "Leila," she said, lying on instinct.

"Let's see if I can get you untied," he said.

She offered him her wrists, and he worked on the rope until he could get the knots undone. The relief when she could move her arms again was enormous. "Oh, that's better," she said. She turned to look at him. "What happened to your head?"

He put a hand up to touch it, a rueful look on his face. "I got separated from my unit. I'm a bit unclear about what actually happened—I think someone conked me on the head, and the next thing I knew, I was here."

"How long have you been here?" Annalie asked.

"Two days."

"Did they get you a doctor?"

"Nothing like that. Why—does it look serious?"

"It's very gory."

"I think head wounds often are. I don't think it's life-threatening, luckily for me. No double vision or anything. Too bad if there was, eh? Most of them don't seem to speak Duxish."

Annalie's initial shock and fear at being trapped with an Admiralty officer—someone she had come to think of as her enemy—began to fade. Lieutenant Cherry seemed pleasant and straightforward, and visibly relieved to have company.

"What are they planning to do with us?" she asked. "Do you know?"

"Well, I assume they're holding us for ransom," Cherry said. "Not that it will do them much good in my case."

"Why not?"

"The Admiralty doesn't pay pirates."

"How are they going to get you back, then?"

"I don't know," Cherry said. "I expect there's a policy, but I don't know what it is yet." He paused. "This is my first year at sea."

"Oh," Annalie said. "That's very bad luck."

"You can say that again," Cherry replied glumly.

Annalie lowered her voice slightly, in case someone was listening. "So what kind of people do you think we're dealing with? Are they violent? Or are they just interested in money?"

Cherry considered this. "I don't know yet," he said. "They've fed me, and no one's threatened me or beaten me up—apart from when they captured me. But if they don't get what they want, that could change."

Annalie thought back to what she'd seen on the boat. The pirates who'd attacked them had seemed determined and disciplined, definitely not amateurs. She guessed that they'd done this many times before. She just wished she knew a bit more about how situations like this ended up.

"What happens to people who get kidnapped by pirates, usually?" she asked.

"Well, that depends," Cherry said. "If you've got family or friends back home who can pay the ransom, I think they usually let you go."

"And what if you don't?" Annalie asked.

Cherry screwed his face up.

Annalie's heart sank.

The pirates left them alone for some time. Eventually, food came: a small bowl of rice each with a few vegetables on top, no cutlery to eat it with, and a mug of sour-tasting tea.

"I've had worse," Cherry confided, eating heartily. He had the look of a young man with a big appetite. His food was gone very quickly.

The sun shining through the gap in the window passed over and the room grew gloomier.

They heard more footsteps outside the door. The man who'd brought the food took the bowls away, and then Red Bandana looked in, pointed at Annalie, and with a jerk of his head indicated that she should follow him.

She looked at Cherry fearfully. "It's going to be all right," he said reassuringly.

Red Bandana escorted Annalie down a winding corridor and into a lounge room furnished with low squashy sofas and many colorful rugs and cushions. Five lavishly-mustached Brundisan men of various ages were lounging on the sofas and talking among themselves; they all turned to look at her curiously when she walked in. Red Bandana left her standing

36

in the middle of the floor and sat down between an older man and a boy.

He spoke, and the boy translated. "Where are you from, and what is your name?"

She could have lied to the pirates, but if they were making ransom demands, how would it help if she pretended to be someone else?

"Annalie Wallace," she said. "I'm from Dux."

Red Bandana and the older man spoke to one another, and the boy translated. "Do you have a family who want you back?"

"Yes," Annalie said.

"If they want you back, they must pay," the boy said.

"My family isn't rich," Annalie explained.

The men laughed when the boy translated this.

"Everyone in Dux is rich. People in Brundisi are poor," the boy said.

"I don't have a rich family," Annalie said.

"You have a boat," the boy said.

Annalie wondered if that meant the pirates hadn't taken the *Sunfish* after all. Could the others have gotten away? "I *had* a boat," she said. "I don't know who's got it now."

"You have a boat, you have money," the boy said. "You can pay a ransom."

Annalie realized the boy's previous remark didn't reveal anything about the current status of the *Sunfish*. All it showed was the assumption they'd made about her, based on the fact that she'd been taken from a privately owned boat. "Okay, sure," she said. "If you'll just give me a shell, I can—"

"*You* don't call," said the boy. "*We* call. You give us names now."

Of *course* they were not going to let her make the call herself.

"I don't have a lot of names to give you," she said. She turned to Red Bandana. "Your people had my friends. I don't know what happened to them after you took me off the boat."

Red Bandana looked affronted at being addressed directly. He looked at the boy for a translation, then snapped something. The boy said, "You don't worry about them. You just give us names."

"Okay," Annalie said. There were only two names she could give them. She gave them Essie's call ID first, then Spinner's, even though she knew there was little chance of them getting through to him. She just had to hope that Essie wasn't locked up in another room like this one—or worse.

"What happens if you can't get hold of them?" she asked. "Or they can't pay?"

"You don't leave here until someone pays," the boy said. "In the end, someone always pays."

Doria

Will, Pod, and Essie sailed with all speed for Gantua. They had good winds all the way, and saw no further signs of pirates.

Will's first thought had been to go ashore in the busy port city of Haal, but as they approached, he spotted an Admiralty ship even larger than the one they'd seen in Dio coming in to port. He got the binoculars out and discovered that Haal was home to an Admiralty base, similar in size to the one back in his hometown of Port Fine, and it had a second Admiralty ship already at anchor. Haal was clearly not an option.

They checked the charts, looking for somewhere else to go.

"Ooh—Doria!" said Essie.

"We're not going there," Will said sternly.

"Too dangerous?" asked Pod.

"No, it's supposed to be beautiful," Essie said wistfully. "Me and my parents were talking about going there for a holiday next summer. Of course," she added wryly, "that was before my dad got arrested and my mum left him for a shipping magnate. I don't suppose we'll be going now."

Doria was once a fabled holiday destination on the far east coast of Gantua, with clear blue waters, white sandy beaches, amazing snorkeling, dolphins, whales, sea turtles and fish, and a deepwater harbor that made it perfect for cruise ships. The town had hotels and resorts, clubs and restaurants, markets and palaces and temples and shopping. The Flood had washed much of it away, but Gantua was so dependent on the money that came in from Doria's tourist trade that it was rebuilt almost as splendidly as before. And while the dolphins and sea turtles were never seen these days, the beaches had been meticulously replaced with brand new sand brought in from elsewhere, new hotels and restaurants had gone up, and Doria was almost as lively a tourist destination as it had ever been.

Spinner had always disapproved of places like Doria because he believed that when there were so many places crying out to be rebuilt, it was almost wicked to spend so much money on a playground for the rich. There was, of course, an argument that places like Doria were important and necessary because they kept the local people in work, and without the tourist trade, they would have no way of making a living. Spinner conceded that, but disliked it for the way it seemed to represent the vast gulf between the people who could afford to come to a place like Doria and all the other people who couldn't.

Will had dismissed Doria for all these reasons, but in the present circumstances, he could see it might be exactly what they were looking for.

"Maybe it wouldn't be such a bad choice," he conceded. "There are lots of foreigners there, so we wouldn't be so obvious, and plenty of boat traffic, too. Hopefully it'll be easy to slip in and out unnoticed."

And so they sailed on to Doria. As they drew close to the harbor, Essie's shell pinged, and they all came together to see what the message was.

An unidentified caller had rung, but had left no message.

"Do you think that was them?" Will asked.

"It could be," Essie said.

"Call them back," Will said.

"I can't," Essie said. "That's what 'No call ID' means."

Will frowned, stymied. "Why wouldn't they leave a message?" he asked.

"I don't know," Essie said.

"Only want to talk directly?" Pod suggested.

Will looked at the others. "What do we do? What if they call again?"

"If they call again, I'll answer them," Essie said. "We can't do anything until we know what they want. And we still need to find a vet for Graham."

They sailed into Doria's harbor and dropped anchor in a distant corner. Pod and Essie took the dinghy and went ashore with Graham while Will stayed with the boat. They promised to call him if they heard anything more from the pirates.

It was getting close to the end of the tourist season in Doria, but to Pod it seemed amazingly crowded. They walked at first through strolling, shopping throngs of Duxans and northerners, past gleaming shops and fashionable restaurants that made Essie sigh with longing; then they moved beyond the tourist areas and into the backstreets where the ordinary Gantuans lived and worked. Eventually they found their way to the vet clinic Essie's shell had identified. The receptionist didn't speak Duxan or either of the other two languages Essie could get by in, but when they showed him Graham's wing, it was clear what they needed.

The vet was summoned; she showed them into an examination room and looked at Graham's wound. Luckily, she could speak a little Duxan. "Your parrot need surgery," she explained, reaching for the right words. "To fix, must be ..." She mimed being asleep.

"You can't just sew him up?" Pod asked, miming sewing.

The vet made a see-sawing motion with her hand, a dubious expression on her face. "Surgery ... better," she said.

"If he has the surgery, will he be able to fly again?"

"I think," the vet said.

"And if he doesn't?"

The vet raised her eyebrows skeptically.

Pod and Essie looked at each other. "I guess he needs the surgery, then," Pod said.

Graham—who was under instructions not to speak—squawked, although it wasn't clear if he was approving or objecting.

"There will be cost," the vet warned gently. She had evidently noted the state of their clothes. Essie's had once been expensive and fashionable, but months on the boat had taken their toll, and now they were worn and salt-stained. Pod's clothes had never been nice. No one could have blamed her for wondering if they could pay their bill.

"We can pay," Essie said confidently. "Can you tell us how much it's going to be, please?"

The vet quickly added up the costs for the surgery, the anesthesia, and the medicines. Essie choked when she saw the total.

"Is that in Duxan creds?" she asked.

"Of course," the vet said.

Essie looked at Pod anxiously, then pulled him into the corner. "This will use up all of our money," she whispered. "And once it's gone, I don't know how we'll get any more."

They both turned to look at Graham, who was sitting on the examination table, his damaged wing drooping. His handsome plumage was dull and ruffled; he looked miserable and frightened.

"He needs the surgery," Pod said.

"But it's so much money," Essie said. "And what if we need it to pay the pirates?"

Pod scowled unhappily.

Essie looked at Graham, then at the vet, and came to a decision. "I've got an idea," she said. "Stay here with Graham. I'll be back as soon as I can."

Essie was gone for nearly two hours. Pod sat in the waiting room with the grumbling, unhappy Graham. He had no idea what Essie had in mind, and he didn't feel entirely comfortable about having let her wander off alone into yet another strange town. Admittedly, this one was less scary than some of the places they'd been, but he also knew that tourist towns were magnets for villains and thieves who knew tourists were easy pickings. He began to wish he'd gone with her so he could keep her safe, but that would have meant leaving Graham alone, and he couldn't really do that either. Frustrated and cross with himself, he squirmed in his seat and kept hopping up to look for Essie out the window until even Graham told him to sit still. ("Pod got ants in pants?")

At last the door to the waiting room opened and Essie appeared. "I've got it," she said, looking triumphant but a little shaky.

The vet was summoned back. "We've got the money," Essie told her. "When can he have the surgery?"

Graham was whisked away and the two of them sat down to wait once again.

"How did you get it?" Pod asked quietly when the receptionist was out of the room. "Rob a bank?"

Essie shook her head, and then pulled a shell from her pocket. Pod looked at it uncomprehendingly.

"I sold my old shell and headset," Essie explained. "I had to shop around a bit to get the best price for it—that's why I took so long. The first guy offered me a pittance. It was ridiculous, really. I knew I could do better. So I shopped it around and I ended up getting a pretty good price." She paused. "I don't think I realized before, but shells don't hold their value. As soon as they're not new anymore, the price plunges. But my headset was a limited edition. They're quite rare, so I did okay out of that."

Pod looked at her curiously. "Are you crying?"

"No," Essie said crossly, wiping her eyes.

"It was just a shell."

"I know," Essie said, "but I really liked it. And my dad gave it to me for my birthday." The shell she'd sold had truly been a dazzling object: light, tiny, splendidly fast. It also had the very latest headset, a sleek, jeweled headband with a customizable light display (it flashed and sparkled and you could change the colors to match your outfit) which housed technology that could project the contents of your shell directly in front of your eyes. When it was new, it was the very latest version, and all her friends agreed that it was superior to any other on the market. Her replacement shell was older and fatter and slower and uglier, and did not come with a headset. "This one will do what I need it to do," she sighed.

"That's all you need then," said Pod, who was immune to the magical attraction of shells and did not really appreciate the scale of her sacrifice.

They settled in to wait.

Several more hours passed. The pirates did not call.

Eventually, the vet appeared once again.

"Surgery go well," she said with a smile. "Parrot going to be okay. We keep here, tonight?"

"We'd rather take him with us now, if that's okay," Pod said.

Graham was handed back to them, still groggy from the anesthetic, with some very expensive medicine and instructions about how to change his dressing. They carried him through the darkening streets in a box; occasionally, his blue head would pop out.

"Where Pod?"

"I'm right here, Graham."

"Where going?"

"We're going back to the *Sunfish*."

"On the wet?"

"Yes, on the wet."

"Hate wet."

"I know."

The blue head subsided.

Later it popped up again.

"Where Pod?"

"I'm still here, Graham."

"This storm very rough."

"You're not in a storm. You're in a box."

Graham looked about and saw he was right.

"Hate box."

"You have to be in the box. You can't stand up properly yet."

"Graham wonky?"

"Yes, you are."

Graham looked at Pod imperiously. "Pod be more careful with box."

"Yes, master," Pod said, with a roll of his eyes.

Later, when they were in the dinghy and heading back to the *Sunfish*, Graham popped up one more time. "Pod?"

"Yes, Graham?"

"Pod good friend."

Pod smiled. "Thanks, buddy. You too."

The room

"What have you been able to work out about this place?" Annalie asked. "Do you know where we are? Is there any way to get out?"

"I *think* we're still in Dio," Cherry said. "At least, that's where I was taken from, and I assume they wouldn't have taken me somewhere else. Not that that helps us very much. I don't know how much you know about Dio, but the place is enormous."

"Right," Annalie said vaguely. Nice as Cherry was, she had decided to let him know as little as possible about who she was, what she knew, and where she was going. "What about this room, did you search it? Is there any way out of here?"

"I don't think so," Cherry said. "Apart from the door."

Annalie got up to have a look. "It's not that I don't believe you," she said apologetically. "I just want to see for myself."

Looking around, she guessed the room had originally been a bedroom, perhaps a child's room, because it was quite small. The walls were bare now, but different-colored patches showed where furniture had once been, decorations too. She got up on tiptoe and tried the boards over the window.

"I couldn't budge them," Cherry said.

"I don't suppose you've got a pocket knife on you?" Annalie asked. They were part of a sailor's standard kit.

"I *had* one," Cherry said. "They took it off me."

Will always carried a pocket knife about with him too, but Annalie never had. She made a mental note that if she ever got herself out of this mess, she would get one.

"It's not going to be easy getting those boards off, then," she said.

"Wouldn't be much help if we could," Cherry said. "That window's tiny."

Annalie had to admit he was right; the window was so small not even she could have crept through it. She stood on tiptoe and looked out the little gap between the boards. The viewing angle was narrow and showed only the weatherbeaten walls of a neighboring house, featureless and sheer, with nothing to climb up, no windows to signal to, and no glimpse of any landmarks which might help them work out where they were.

She turned back to the room and studied it thoroughly. She tried the door, just in case—locked; checked the ceiling for hatches or trapdoors—none; looked around the walls for a concealed door or window—nothing.

"Anything under the mat?" she asked.

Cherry rolled off it obligingly and let her pull it aside. There was, of course, nothing to see underneath.

Restlessly, Annalie paced around the room, looking, listening, feeling. In one corner, she felt the boards give under her feet. She bounced experimentally and the floorboards bounced with her.

"I think a joist's gone," Cherry observed.

"Any idea what's underneath?"

"Wouldn't have a clue."

Annalie bounced one more time and then went back to sit on the floor.

"So there's no obvious way out," Cherry said.

"No," Annalie said.

"And whenever they come to the door, they tend to do it in pairs," Cherry said, "so I don't like our chances of overpowering them. Unless you're a master of the defensive arts?"

"I'm not really one for fighting," Annalie said.

"Are you not?" he said, and smiled. "Don't worry. We'll get out of here. One way or another."

"Do you have a plan?" she asked hopefully.

"My people will come for me," Cherry said. "We never leave anyone behind. I'll make sure we take you with us."

"Oh," Annalie said, rather deflated.

"Rescuing people is what we do," Cherry said.

Annalie gave him what she hoped was a grateful smile, and said nothing.

When the sun went down, the room became utterly dark, and remained dark for a long time. Cherry eventually dozed off, but Annalie lay awake, listening to the sounds around her. She could hear the rattle and clatter of domestic life, both within the building and outside the walls: people cooking and talking, eating and laughing, babies crying and being soothed by their mothers. It made her feel sad and lonely and homesick. She wondered if she would ever see her brother, her friends or her father again. To distract herself, she listened to the putter of dinghies and the slap of water against walls outside, and decided her earlier guess was probably correct: that they were holed up somewhere in the part of Dio with its feet in the water. Cherry snored gently; the moon came out and a thin silver glow crept into the room. The sounds of the city quieted, and Annalie, lying with her head close to the floorboards, could hear a sound coming up from below: the gentle boom of water lapping at internal walls. A waterlogged room lay below them. And perhaps where the water could come in, there might be a way for a determined person to get out.

Another buyer

Annalie woke to the jolting of floorboards. Cherry was up and doing his morning exercises. She recognized them at once: the Admiralty had compulsory calisthenics first thing in the morning, and they'd been one of her least favorite parts of the Triumph College curriculum.

Noticing that she was awake, Cherry grinned at her. "Exercise before breakfast. It's the best way to start the day. It always helps put me in a positive state of mind."

"Even here?" Annalie said skeptically.

"*Especially* here," Cherry said.

He switched from star jumps to push-ups. "Feel free to join me," he said. He was barely puffing.

"Thanks, but I'll pass," Annalie said.

"We need to stay in peak condition if we're going to escape," he said.

Annalie suspected he was teasing her. "You can't blame a girl for trying," she said.

"I don't blame you at all," Cherry said. "I admire your spirit."

His arms pumped up and down like pistons. "Tell

me," he said, "what brought you out here? The Sea of Brundisi is a pretty dangerous place to be."

"We were on our way to somewhere else," Annalie said. "Pirates attacked us."

"At sea?"

Annalie nodded.

"What kind of vessel were you in?"

"My father has a boat," Annalie said, a little awkwardly. "It's only a little one."

"No such thing as too little for these guys," Cherry said. "So they chased you? Boarded you?"

Annalie nodded again. "We tried to fight back, but then I was taken hostage."

"What happened to your friends?" Cherry asked.

"I don't know," Annalie said. Suddenly her eyes were full of tears. "I don't know if they were captured, or—"

Cherry stopped his exercising and looked concerned. "Who was on the boat with you? Your family?"

"Family and friends," Annalie said, her voice wobbly. "Almost everyone I care about, actually."

Cherry looked at her with sympathy. "They might have gotten away."

"Do you think so?" she asked.

"Sure," Cherry said. "It happens."

But she could see he was lying.

She turned her head away. She didn't want him to see her cry.

Later that morning, Red Bandana came for her again. This time there were just three men in the lounge room: Red Bandana, the older man, and the boy. Red Bandana spoke first; he was in a bad mood.

"You give us more names," the boy translated, echoing Red Bandana's aggressive tone.

"I don't have any more names to give you," Annalie said.

"We called. They don't answer," the boy said. "Where are they?"

"I told you, I don't know," Annalie said. She turned to Red Bandana. "Your friends know where they are."

Red Bandana shouted at her and waved his hand angrily.

"You have to give us more names," the boy said. "Or we start looking for another buyer."

Another buyer? What did that mean? Annalie wondered, worried. "Try them again, *please.* I don't know where they are, they might just be out of range, but you've got to keep trying. I know they want me back. We don't have much money, but whatever we can get, we'll give you, I promise."

"You give us more names. Dux people."

"I don't know any more people, I really don't," Annalie said.

Red Bandana and the older man conferred, then gave the boy instructions. "We don't talk to them today, you're in big trouble," the boy said.

"You won't like it," Cherry said. "But they're probably talking about selling you to a slaver."

"Oh," Annalie said.

"They won't get as much money for you," he continued, "but it's better than nothing." He paused. "It may sound scary, but it's actually kind of comforting. This is a business to these guys. They don't *want* to hurt or kill you. They just want to make some money from you—as much money as possible. They don't really care where it comes from as long as you're worth something to them."

"You mean they'd sell me to the highest bidder?"

"Yep," Cherry said.

Annalie was stunned. She knew, of course, that Pod had once been a slave, but it had never occurred to her that such a thing could happen to *her*. A shiver of horror ran through her at the thought.

"I'm not saying it's a *good* outcome," Cherry said. "One of my first operations—no, never mind."

"What?" Annalie asked.

Cherry looked at her sideways, considering whether or not to tell her his story.

"I want to hear it," Annalie said.

"We were sent to investigate a factory," Cherry said. "It was in Estilo, but the bad end of Estilo on the Sea of Brundisi. They've got a few towns over there that've set up as manufacturing hubs—they make all kinds of stuff very cheap, and everybody knows it's because they mostly use slave labor. And mostly nobody cares. They pretend to be legit, and their customers pretend not to know how the goods are being made because it's so cheap. Anyway, someone must have made an official complaint, because we were sent to investigate."

He paused. "The factory made bed linen. Sheets, quilt covers. Those flouncy things you put around the bottom of beds. The doors were all chained shut, so none of the workers could escape. They lived in there, worked in there, two shifts, working around the clock. They'd do twelve hours on the machines, then they'd lie down around the edges of the workroom and try to sleep. They were cooking in there too, on little stoves with naked flames—imagine! In a bedding factory! Where there's fabric and lint and fluff and cotton everywhere! You'd only have to knock one of those stoves over and the whole place would go up. The people looked like ghosts. They were so thin and pale—they were never allowed outside—never had a day off, and the food they were getting was pathetic. I've never seen anything like it. But here's the thing—even after we came in and closed the factory down, a lot of them didn't want to leave. They were begging us to let them stay. I couldn't figure it out."

"What were you going to do with them once you let them go?"

"Another ship was going to take them to a refugee camp."

"Ah," said Annalie.

"What do you mean, 'ah'?" asked Cherry, perplexed.

"No one wants to end up in a refugee camp," Annalie said. "You'll live your whole life there with no chance of ever getting out. Those people who wanted to stay must have thought they had at least some chance of a better life there."

"They were locked in, twenty-four hours a day," Cherry said. "The factory was a death trap."

"I've heard the refugee camps aren't too nice, either," Annalie said.

"And anyway, it isn't true you don't have a chance of getting out of the camps," Cherry said stoutly. "People get resettled all the time. Dux has a very active refugee resettlement program."

This was not what Annalie had heard, but she could see that Cherry believed it.

"So do you do a lot of that sort of thing?" she asked.

"What do you mean?"

"Liberating slaves."

Cherry's face brightened. "It's different every day. That's what I like about it."

"You like being in the Admiralty, then?"

"Of course!" he said. "Why else would you join?"

"Well, maybe because you have to if you want to go on and do something else," Annalie suggested.

Cherry just laughed and shook his head. "My family would quite like me to get a nice safe job in an office. But I love being at sea."

"What do you love about it?" Annalie was genuinely curious.

"I like the camaraderie," Cherry said. "And the fact that you never know what you're going to be doing next. When you're out on patrol, you might be chasing pirates or answering a distress call. We've done search and rescue operations. Remember that yacht that got lost, that had the vid star on it?"

Annalie shook her head, mystified.

"You really don't remember? It was all over the newsfeeds."

"I don't pay much attention to those," Annalie mumbled.

"We were part of the search. Wasn't our vessel that found her, unfortunately, but we saw the signal that led to the other guys finding them."

"Wow," Annalie said politely.

"Sometimes we're just sailing up and down, making our presence felt, keeping the bad guys away. And that can be a bit boring. But one of my superior officers told me that it's good when it's boring. It *should* be boring. Because that means you're keeping people safe." He beamed at her.

Annalie looked at him curiously, remembering the stories she'd heard, the things she'd seen with her own eyes. She longed to press him on whether he'd been part of the not-so-noble actions, too—the ones where they burned people's homes or threatened to shoot them. But she couldn't think of a way to bring it up without making him suspicious. So she said nothing.

The morning passed quietly, but as morning became afternoon, one of Red Bandana's companions appeared and waved Annalie vigorously to the door.

"What's he so excited about?" Cherry wondered aloud.

Annalie could only hope it was good news.

Once more she was ushered into the room with the squashy lounges. Red Bandana was there with the boy and the old man, and this time, Red Bandana looked radiantly happy.

"We know who you are," the boy translated.

Red Bandana crowed and shouted something.

"You're a bad girl!" the boy translated. "Why didn't you tell us you're one of us?"

Annalie stared at him, and then realized what had happened. They'd searched her name on the links and found the story about Essie's kidnapping.

"That girl, that heiress. She still on your boat?" the boy asked.

"No," Annalie said. "We lost her."

The boy translated this. Red Bandana shook his head and waved his finger at her in a "naughty naughty" gesture.

"You're lying," the boy translated. "He remember her. She was the other girl on the boat."

"All right, that was her. But there isn't any money," Annalie said. "Didn't you read the story? Her father can't get at his money, and the Duxans won't pay. We already tried. There's no money; she's not worth anything. The whole thing was a bust."

The boy translated this. Red Bandana's expression darkened. He shot out a burst of rapid-fire instructions.

"You don't know how to squeeze a family," the boy said. "*We* could get the money, no problem."

"I promise you, there's no way," Annalie said.

"We think there is," said the boy. He paused while Red Bandana spoke again. "That call ID you gave us, that was her call ID?"

Annalie had to nod—it was pointless to deny it.

"You call her. Get her to come here. If you give her to us, we'll let you go."

"What?"

"You want to get free? Give us the rich girl."

Annalie stared at them, horrified. Swap her freedom for Essie's? Never.

"I already told you," she stalled. "I don't know where she is now. If she's not answering her shell, I have no way of getting in touch with her."

Red Bandana didn't need this translated. He was already talking.

"Then you're no use to us," the boy translated. "We contact the other buyer now." Red Bandana was already reaching for his own shell.

"Wait!" Annalie said, trying not to panic. "Did I give you this call ID?" She reeled off her own.

Red Bandana gave a nasty smirk.

"No, you didn't," the boy said. "Whose is that?"

"It's mine," Annalie said. "I left my shell behind on the boat. Hopefully someone's still there to answer it."

"Your brother?" the boy said. "The other kidnapper?"

"That's the one," Annalie said faintly.

"Will he be willing to talk business?"

"I expect so," Annalie said.

She was taken back to the room, her mind reeling. The pirates knew who she was; they had recognized Essie. The fact that Red Bandana was still hoping to convince the others to hand Essie over to him had to mean that the pirates had not managed to capture the others. They were still free!

This was the first good news she'd had, and she felt a surge of joy as she thought this through. But if they'd managed to escape, where were they now? And why wasn't Essie answering her shell?

She decided not to worry about that. There were a million reasons why that might be, including the most obvious: they were somewhere at sea with no signal.

She hoped it didn't mean they'd given her up for dead and sailed away. But she didn't think they'd do that.

No, they were probably somewhere nearby, planning their next move. For a moment she felt hopeful at the thought that they might be planning a rescue attempt, but that hope was quickly replaced by the *fear* that they might be planning a rescue attempt. If it went wrong, they could all wind up as prisoners.

She wished she could remember exactly what the kidnapping article had actually said. It had certainly mentioned a ransom demand. She didn't *think* there had been anything in there about a reward. Or had there?

If the pirates had smelled the chance of a reward, they wouldn't just be after Essie. They'd want to capture *all* of them.

There would be no exchange, she realized. That was just a ruse to get them all in one place. Then Red Bandana would capture the lot of them and sell them off for as much as he could, to Essie's parents, the Admiralty, the Duxan government—whoever was willing to pay the highest price.

Annalie put her head in her hands, realizing she had just made things a thousand times worse. *Why didn't I lie to them about who I was?* she thought. She'd assumed that, because the pirates were poor, they were technologically backward. But the links worked, even in Brundisi, and information was highly valuable.

I wish there was some way I could talk to the others myself, she thought. *Send them a message. Warn them not to come.*

But she couldn't imagine how she could convince the pirates to let her do that.

"You're very quiet," Cherry said from a corner of the room. She looked up; he was watching her with a rather penetrating look. "How did things go in there? Any new developments?"

Annalie hesitated. There had been plenty, but not many that she wanted to share with an Admiralty officer. "They still haven't been able to contact my friends," she said. "They wanted me to come up with more numbers."

"Did you have any?"

She nodded. "I had to. They were threatening to sell me to this other buyer."

"Is it a real number?"

"It's real, but I don't know how much help they're going to be." She paused. "I think it's possible my friends escaped."

Cherry looked pleased. "That's great! Do you think they'll be able to help you get out of here?"

"I don't know," Annalie said uneasily. "I guess we'll find out."

She lapsed into silence again, returning to her thoughts.

Perhaps she could convince the pirates to pass on a message? Something that would give the others a clue that this was a trap? She thought and thought. Then an idea came to her.

She went and knocked on the door. "Hello! Excuse me! I need to talk to someone!" She kept on banging and calling until the door opened. Red Bandana himself stood there. "We need to talk," Annalie said.

"So you see, my brother still thinks he can get the money out of Essie's parents himself. He doesn't believe it's hopeless. Personally I think it was time to give up months ago. We've done all we can and we failed. So I'm happy to let you have her and see what you can do. But my brother's not going to give her up so easily."

Annalie waited while the boy translated all of this. Red Bandana listened carefully, his frown deepening. When the explanation ended, Annalie continued. "He might agree to hand her over, or *say* he agrees to it. But he won't actually mean it. So when you talk to him, you should tell him Annalie told him to remember Gloradol."

"Remember Gloradol? What does that mean?"

"He'll know what it means." Annalie could see that this explanation did not satisfy them, so she elaborated. "We had a chance to make some money in Gloradol, and he stuffed it up. He won't want to make the same mistake twice." Red Bandana listened to the translation, studying her, his eyes narrowed. Annalie gazed back at him, hoping she sounded convincing. "I don't want this dragging on any more than you do," she said. "Just tell him to remember Gloradol. He'll get the message."

She hoped and prayed she was right.

The trade

"**I**s this Will Wallace?"

"Yes," Will said cautiously. The *Sunfish* rode at anchor in Doria harbor. The three of them plus Graham were gathered around Annalie's shell.

"We have your sister," said the voice on the shell. "Do you want her back?"

"Of course."

"It will cost you."

"How much?"

"You have a nice boat. She's a smart girl. Worth a lot of money, we think."

"How much?" Will asked again.

"A hundred thousand Duxan creds," the voice said.

Will almost choked. "*How much*? How do you expect me to get my hands on that much money?"

"If you want your sister back, you'd better try," the voice said.

"We're not rich people," Will said. "Is there—is there any chance we could negotiate on the price?"

"Sure," the voice said. "You pay less than the full amount, maybe you don't get all of your sister back. But we can negotiate."

"No, please don't hurt her! We want all of her back."

"Then you'd better find the money," the voice said. There was a pause, then it said, "Unless ..."

"Unless what?" Will said eagerly.

"We know that you have a passenger on board. An heiress."

Essie's eyes widened in surprise.

"Do you still have her?"

"Why do you want to know?"

"If you still have her, we might be willing to make a trade. Your sister for the rich girl."

Pod was making vigorous "no" gestures with his hands. Essie simply looked aghast.

"What if we don't want to make that trade?" Will asked.

"Then it's simple," the voice said. "You pay us a hundred thousand Duxan credits."

Will's brain felt like a wet sheet flapping in the wind. He tried to gather his wits. "Okay, okay, suppose we *were* willing to make the trade, you'd just give my sister back, no questions asked, no money changing hands, just a straight swap?"

"Straight swap," the voice said.

Essie gave Will an outraged look.

"And—and where would the exchange take place?" Will asked.

"We will name the place," the voice said.

Pod was shaking his head at Will.

"I'm sure—I'm sure something could be arranged," Will said, desperately scrambling for something, anything he could use. "Where are you?"

"We will tell you the location later," the voice said. "But remember: if the trade doesn't go smoothly, if we think you're trying to double-cross us, your sister dies."

"I wouldn't," Will said. "Double-cross you. Of course I wouldn't."

"We want the rich girl. We don't want your sister. If you want your sister back, then remember Gloradol, and do what we say."

"Sorry—*what* did you say?"

"Remember Gloradol. Your sister said you'd know what that means." The voice paused for a moment, then said, "We'll call you with further instructions tomorrow at five. Be ready."

The call ended abruptly.

Will and the others stared at each other in shock.

"'Remember Gloradol'?" Essie said. "What do you think it means?"

"Annalie's trying to send us a message," Pod said.

"Gloradol trap," Graham said.

"You're right," Will said. "It was a trap. Maybe this is, too."

"What does she want us to do, then?" Essie said.

"Not go," Graham said. "Stupid girl."

"But we have to go," Pod said.

"Obviously," said Will.

"Wait, wait," Essie said. This was all getting too gung-ho too fast for her taste. "Shouldn't we try and go to the police? See if they can help us?"

"'Hello, corrupt Brundisan policeman. My name's Will, and I'm a wanted kidnapper. Could you help

67

me find my sister, the other wanted kidnapper?'" Will said sarcastically.

"There are police here in Doria, too," Essie said. "But you're right, the kidnap story means we can't go to the authorities."

"So we're just going to have to try and come up with a plan," Will said.

"Or the money," Essie said.

"A hundred thousand creds?" Will said, laughing incredulously.

"Maybe we could sell some stuff, raise the money that way," Pod suggested. "There's good stuff here on the boat. It must be worth something."

"This is a bunch of secondhand junk. It's worth nothing," Will said scornfully.

"What do you suppose the boat's worth?" Pod asked.

"We're not selling the boat," Will snapped.

"She's your sister," Pod said.

They glared at each other. Will was the first to break his gaze. "I don't really know what it's worth," he finally muttered. "I don't know if it'd fetch a hundred. Maybe, if we were lucky. Doria's the kind of place where you might be able to sell a boat ..." He shook off the idea, looking accusingly at Pod. "But then we'd be trapped here."

"We'd have Annalie back," Pod countered.

Essie didn't like the thought that had come to her, but knew she had to say it. "Maybe we should just let them take me," she said in a wobbly voice.

"Don't be stupid," Will said. "We're not handing

you over, and we're going to get Annalie back. We just
have to come up with a plan."

Coming up with a plan did not turn out to be easy.
One thing they did agree on was that they should
stay in Doria, where they were relatively safe, rather
than heading back to Brundisi. Will would have
preferred to be somewhere near Dio in case they
needed to move quickly, but even he could see
that the risks of this outweighed the benefits. All
around them, enormous yachts worth millions of
creds rode gently at anchor; there were many people
in Doria for whom a hundred thousand creds was
just play money. Will suggested, not quite jokingly,
that they do a midnight raid on a few of the yachts
and see what they could scoop up in the form of
saleable loot.

Essie contributed little to their increasingly wild
plans, and eventually she wandered off to think.
Money was the only answer to this problem, that
much seemed clear, and she was the only one who
had any chance of getting her hands on it. But how?

The creditstream her father had given her had
been closed down. Her father's own bank accounts
had been frozen, and even if he did have some secret
money stashed away somewhere, she thought it was
very likely his communications were being monitored,
so if she tried to send him a message, the Admiralty
would soon find out.

She knew she had a trust fund of her own, but she had no idea how much money was in it and no way of accessing it. The point of trust funds was that the money was kept for you, in trust, and was hard to get at. Her father might be able to get to it, just possibly, but again, she would have to get a message to him first.

Her mother's accounts hadn't been frozen. She had a new fiancé, a shipping magnate with even more money than Everest Wan. But Essie couldn't bring herself to ask her mother. She was still too angry at her for abandoning her father, and the thought of groveling to her for money was sickening. She didn't even think there'd be any point. She could imagine making her case—begging, pleading—and then at the end of it having her mother say, "She's no friend of yours if she gets you into this sort of trouble. And how does it benefit anyone to give money to criminals? Anyway, it isn't my money to spend, it belongs to my fiancé. I'm sorry, but the answer is no."

If only there was some way to get a message to her father through unconventional channels. Pay someone to deliver a message by hand. Tie a note to Graham's leg and get him to fly to Dux. Not that he could actually fly yet. She might as well put a message in a bottle.

Then she had a sudden, brilliant idea.

She whipped out her shell and began flicking through all the screens and screens of funks. Yes! On the sixth screen, among the old weird funks she never used and the outgrown games she never played, was the little blue monster-faced funk she was looking for.

My Monster. She clicked on it, hoping it wasn't so old that it had stopped working, but no: it opened.

My Monster was an old toy she'd had when she was very little. It was a talking monster which rolled its eyes and walked and did tricks. It came with its own funk, and had been designed to interface with other toys and other people. For kids who were too young to be able to type, it had a series of pre-written messages you could send to your parents' shell, things like *I think you're grrrrrrreat!* and *I love you furry much!* and the My Monster catchphrase *I love you so much I want to EAT YOU UP!* It would also let you type your own messages.

When Essie was little, she had sent endless monster-love messages to her father, who had always replied to them. The messages didn't go to his normal message service. They only showed up in the funk itself. She just hoped that Everest, like her, hadn't got around to cleaning all the old funks off his shell, because if he hadn't, she might be able to sneak a message to him that way.

Typing fast, she started explaining her situation, trying to make the most convincing case she could for getting him to send her some money. The Monster Messages were quite short, so she had to do a series of them to get all the details in. But soon enough they were written and sent, each with a little monster growl notification sound.

They didn't bounce back. Essie hoped that was a good sign. Several minutes passed and nothing happened. Her initial excitement began to fade.

Perhaps this had been a stupid idea after all. Everest Wan was a grown-up. Why on earth would he have kept a stupid funk like My Monster on his shell? Disappointment stealing over her, Essie put her shell back in her pocket.

Some hours later, Essie was startled by a growl. Then another. And another.

She picked up her shell and let out a cry of joy.

A string of messages had appeared on My Monster.

Essie my darling! I've been so worried! Of

New message: *course I'll help you and Annalie if I can. But*

New message: *are you sure paying the ransom is the only*

New message: *way to get her back? Have you talked to the*

New message: *authorities? I can make enquiries here about the*

New message: *best way to proceed. There may be other avenues*

New message: *we can pursue. I want to make sure you're safe and*

New message: *not putting yourself into even bigger danger.*

New message: *Love Daddy.*

Essie read his reply with frustration and anxiety. She wrote back at once: *I suppose you've seen the story about me*

New message: *being kidnapped? Which is NOT TRUE. If we*

New message: *go to the authorities for help they'll arrest my*

New message: *friends and I don't want that. Annalie would*

New message: *do anything for me and I have to help her and*

New message: *this is the only way I can think of. Please if you*

New message: *can find a way to send me the money please please*

New message: *do it I will pay you back I promise only please*

New message: *help us. Love Essie xxx*

There was a long pause.

Then an answer came.

I'll see what I can do. Dad x

The dark hole

"Good news," the boy said to Annalie. "Your brother made the deal. Tomorrow we will make the trade. And then you will be free."

Annalie's eyes slid to Red Bandana. He was smiling like the cat that had got the cream. She didn't like that smile. "Did you tell him what I said? Remember Gloradol?"

"We told him. He understood. He said there will be no problems."

Red Bandana spoke up. The boy translated. "Be happy. Your time with us is almost up." Red Bandana laughed, a scary laugh that made Annalie feel more certain than ever that the pirates were up to no good.

Why didn't they listen? she thought frantically as she was escorted back to the room once more. *I warned them not to come. Why are they coming? Oh, I bet they've got some idiotic scheme to rescue me.*

She was taken back to the room. Cherry looked up as the door locked behind her. "So what's the story?"

"They spoke to my family," Annalie said, too agitated to keep it to herself. "They said they're coming to collect me tomorrow."

Cherry looked both happy for her and slightly crestfallen. "That's wonderful news. It means you're getting out of here."

"I'm not sure that it does," Annalie said. "I think they're just trying to lure the others here so they can catch them too and then hold all of us for ransom."

Cherry looked a little puzzled as he thought through what she'd said. "I thought you said your family didn't have much money. Why would they want to capture more of you?"

Annalie could see him trying to put the pieces together. Too late, she remembered that he had probably been briefed on her family. "It doesn't matter," she said hurriedly. "Who knows what they're really up to?"

"You said you were traveling with family and friends," Cherry said slowly. "Who are your friends?"

Annalie decided to simply ignore his question. "The problem is they're coming, even though I tried to warn them to stay away," she said. "We have to find a way out of here. Tonight."

Cherry's eyebrows shot up. "There isn't a way out."

"What about that bouncy board in the floor?"

Cherry looked at her askance.

"It's already weakened. Maybe if we both worked on it we might find a way to get through."

"But we don't know what's underneath," Cherry said.

"There's water underneath."

"How do you know?"

"I listened. You can hear it."

75

Cherry's expression changed. He was actually considering the idea.

"Let's at least try," Annalie said.

Together, they went to the corner of the room where the floor sagged. The boards were all in place, but when you stood on them, they flexed.

"Be easier if we had some tools," Cherry mused. "A blade or a lever—"

"But we don't," Annalie said. "Maybe if I stand on one—or you stand on it, you're heavier—we might be able to pry one loose. Then it'll be easier to get the next one up."

They focused their efforts on the board that moved the most. First they tried prying it up, but that didn't work. "Let's try this the old-fashioned way," Cherry said. He bounced and bounced on the board until it snapped right through. "Now we're getting somewhere," he said with a grin.

Once they had one gap in the boards, it was easier to make more. Annalie and Cherry worried away at the gaps, forcing up the old floorboards, using the broken piece as a lever. The damp conditions meant the boards were not in the greatest shape to begin with; it took them some time, but at last they managed to make themselves a hole big enough to wriggle through.

Both of them peered down. It was perfectly dark down there, and an evil smell of rot and old seawater exhaled through the gap.

"Wish we had a flashlight," Cherry said, looking down into the darkness with trepidation. "I wonder how deep it is?"

"Can you swim?" Annalie asked.

Cherry nodded. "You?"

"Yes."

"All right, then," Cherry said. "No more mucking around. I'd better go first, eh?"

"I can—"

But he was already lowering himself down. His feet touched water before his head had even disappeared below the level of the floor. "Water level's high," he reported, rather nervously. "I'm going to let go now. If this is the last you hear from me, don't follow."

He let go. Annalie heard a splash, surprisingly loud. She froze, wondering if the occupants of the house might have heard it too. But there were no sounds from outside; no one came to see what they were up to. "Cherry?" she called softly. "Are you all right?"

"Yes," he replied breathlessly. "Water's quite deep, though. I can't touch the bottom."

"Can you see a way out?"

"Can't see a thing."

Annalie hesitated on the edge, then reminded herself that it was just a room, an ordinary room, even if it was full of water. It must have a door somewhere. If she wanted to escape, this was the only way out. "I'm coming down," she said.

She eased herself down into the hole. The air felt cold and cave-like; the smell seemed to press in upon her. She dropped into water that was cold and slimy, touched the bottom and pushed back up to the surface, gasping. Cherry found her, and she grabbed his forearm, treading water.

"We need to find a way out," she panted.

They paddled together until they touched a wall. "Feel along it," Cherry said. "We'll try and find an opening."

They tried, but the wall was blank and featureless. As they paddled into a corner, Annalie felt something slither across her legs. She screamed, unable to stop herself.

"What's wrong?" said Cherry hoarsely.

"Something swam over my legs," she said.

Cherry froze. "What sort of something?"

"I don't know."

"Something sharky?"

"More—tentacley," Annalie said.

"Like an octopus?"

"Maybe it was just seaweed."

"Yes," Cherry said. "I hope so."

They redoubled their efforts, working their way along the second wall, afraid to touch anything, afraid to drift apart, worried now that there might be something in there with them, something hostile, lurking in the dark water.

"There has to be a door," Annalie said, "but I can't feel anything."

"What if they blocked it off to try to keep the water out?" Cherry suggested.

"Why would they do something that stupid?" Annalie said anxiously. "There must be a door. We just have to find it."

They kept working their way around the second wall.

"I feel something!" Cherry said.

Annalie's hands found it too: a doorframe. They traced the shape in the darkness.

"Where's the handle?"

"I can feel it with my knee," Annalie said.

"We're going to have to try and get it open," Cherry said.

Annalie could sense his hesitation. "Is something the matter?" she asked.

"It's just that I'm not terribly good at putting my head underwater," Cherry said awkwardly.

"I thought you said you could swim!"

"Well, I passed swimming proficiency in basic training. But before that I hadn't had much experience in the water."

Annalie didn't know whether to be impressed by how game he was, or annoyed at the thought he was much less skilled than she'd imagined.

"It's all right," she said. "I'll go."

Cherry started to say something, but Annalie was already ducking under the water. She grabbed the handle firmly; it turned, but the door wouldn't move. She came to the surface again to take a deeper breath, then went back down. She turned the handle, pushed, pulled, wiggled and jiggled. Still the door would not budge.

She came back up. "I can't get it open," she said. "The handle turns, but the door won't open."

There was a brief pause. "Okay," Cherry said. "Let me try."

There was another long pause, and she heard him breathing in the darkness. Then he gulped an enormous breath and went under. She could feel him fighting with the door as he struggled to get it open—he had no more success than she did. He came up, gasping loudly for breath. "It's no use," he said. "Either the wood's too swollen from all the water, or there's something pressed against it. Debris, too much water. Who knows. I think we might be stuck here."

She could hear the note of fear in his voice. "It's okay," she said. "We'll just look for another way out. There could be a window. Which way are we facing? Do you remember which way was the outer wall?"

"Er—I think it was this way," Cherry said.

They paddled on to the third wall and continued to feel their way along.

"Can you feel that?" Annalie said suddenly.

"What?" Cherry said, his voice taut with fear.

"It felt like a current."

She had felt the surge of water around her legs. The water in the room was moving, just slightly. "I think there could be a gap in the wall somewhere," she said. "Let's find it."

They felt around the wall above the water line, but found nothing that indicated a window. Annalie felt the water sucking back gently around her legs. She took another breath and dived down, feeling her way down the wall—and there it was. A hole in the wall, at the old floor level.

"I've found it," she said, "our way out. There's

a hole in the wall. If this is the outer wall, it should lead outside."

"But we don't know what's on the other side," Cherry protested. "What if we swim through it and there's no way out? We could get trapped there."

Annalie could hear his fear, and now that he'd said it, she found herself imagining nightmare scenarios: going down into the hole and getting stuck, or swimming through it into somewhere worse, darker, enclosed, being unable to get out ...

"I think this is our best way out," she said firmly. "I'll go first and see where it leads, and if it doesn't go anywhere, I'll just come back."

"But—" he began, his voice ragged with fear.

"It'll be okay," she said.

She took a deep, deep breath, and dived.

Down into the hole with its ragged sides. The tide swept in, pushing her back into the room so she had to kick hard to keep going. She felt the hole's rough edges scrape her arm as she pushed through into a blackness no less profound than the darkness she'd left behind, and for a moment she feared she had merely swum from one dark hole into another. What if they'd got themselves turned around in the dark and she was swimming into a maze that went on and on, rooms opening onto flooded rooms with no way out? And still she kept swimming, swimming, her heart pounding harder, her lungs starting to strain, and now the tide surged the other way, sweeping her away from the hole, and she had no choice but to kick her way to the surface. She swam up, desperate to breathe, afraid that at any moment she might hit some barrier that would prevent her from reaching the fresh air—and then suddenly she was on the surface, sucking in a huge grateful breath, and when she wiped the salty water from her eyes, she saw the night sky littered with stars. She was free!

Cherry

Soon enough, Annalie and Cherry were both outside, bobbing on the surface.

"I don't think I could have done this without you," Cherry said.

"'Course you could," Annalie said. "You're an Admiralty man." She looked around her. "Any idea where we are?"

They both looked around. They were in that part of Dio where the buildings were as much under the water as above it.

"Not really," Cherry said, "but I know we need to get out of here as quick as we can."

They paddled over to a rickety boardwalk and climbed out. Cherry took his Admiralty jacket off and carried it, but even without the jacket, their Duxan clothes made them both conspicuous.

"How long do you think we've got until they realize we're missing?" Annalie asked.

"I don't know," Cherry said. "Depends on whether we're lucky or unlucky. We need to find ourselves a ride out of here."

They hurried along the boardwalk, listening

for any sounds of pursuit. The path swerved down toward the water; a cluster of dinghies were pulled up above the tideline.

"What's your position on stealing things?" Annalie asked.

"Normally I'm against it," Cherry said. "But in some situations, it's necessary."

He tried the dinghies one by one while Annalie kept a lookout. The first four engines had been disabled and wouldn't start.

Annalie noticed someone opposite had stopped and was watching them. "Maybe we need to keep moving," she said nervously.

Vrroom! The fifth dinghy started. "Let's go!" Cherry said.

They both jumped in. Cherry opened the throttle and drove out into the channel. Behind them, a window was thrown open and somebody shouted furiously, but the voice was quickly lost.

They motored out, making for open water, Annalie keeping watch behind them while Cherry steered a course.

"Anybody following us?" he asked.

"Not yet," Annalie said, half-expecting that at any moment someone would come shooting out to hunt them down.

But no, not this time.

They crossed the debris field and reached the safety of the open ocean. Cherry turned east and they began to put the great sprawl of Dio behind them.

"We made it," he said. "I can't believe it."

"Don't you do this kind of thing all the time?" Annalie asked, smiling.

"Not by myself," Cherry said. "So had you thought about what happens next?"

"I need to get in touch with my friends," Annalie said.

"That's easy," Cherry said. "I'll just take us back to my ship and we can contact them for you."

"That isn't necessary," Annalie said hastily. "I really just need to get my hands on a shell, then I can call them and get them to come and pick me up. Maybe if you dropped me somewhere, and lent me some money to get another shell—"

"I don't have any money," Cherry said. "Or even any ID. I really think we'd be better off going back to my ship."

"There's no time," Annalie said desperately. "I've got to warn my friends not to rendezvous with the pirates before it's too late."

"Then we can stop in at the nearest port and I'll make contact with my ship that way," Cherry said reasonably. "We'll make landfall in Gantua—it's probably safer there. And I can get us both the help we need."

Annalie reluctantly nodded her agreement. She was going to need Cherry's help for just a little longer; once she'd contacted the others, she would simply escape again.

They puttered on over the quiet sea, moving eastward. Cherry seemed to know which way he was going. "You should try to get some rest," he suggested

85

at one point. But Annalie didn't dare. She wanted to make sure she was awake and ready when they finally did reach port.

The hours passed. The dark bulk of Brundisi slipped by, dotted with only a very few lights. The engine droned on. Then more lights began to appear on the shore, more boats on the water. "I think," Cherry said at last, "we're in Gantua."

Annalie sat up a little straighter. Now for the next part in her escape plan. Not that she actually had a plan of any kind.

As the sun rose, they came upon a port town. "This looks like a good place to stop," Cherry said.

It was not a big town. It sat at the mouth of a river, and Annalie guessed the town was a staging point for goods that arrived by sea and then were sent inland by river. Even so, it had a rather sleepy look to it. She hoped that meant it would be easier for her to slip away unnoticed.

There were a number of boats anchored in the harbor, none of them Admiralty. Cherry drove past them all and came to a stop directly in front of the harbormaster's office, shrugging back into his uniform jacket. Annalie followed him slowly. Should she make a run for it? But no—if she did that, she had no way of contacting the others. Better to stick with Cherry for now and get help.

"Good morning," Cherry said to the woman at the front desk. "Do you speak Duxish?"

She stared at him for a moment in surprise, then said, "A little."

"My name is Lieutenant Cherry, and I was kidnapped in Dio by pirates. I managed to escape, along with my friend here, and I need help to get back to my ship."

The woman blinked at him a moment longer, then got down to business. "What is your name, please?"

Annalie stood and listened while Cherry started spouting details: name, rank, number. She was jolted when he named his ship: the *Triumph*. Annalie's boarding school, Triumph College, was the battleship's feeder school. She had been aboard the ship once; it had been an impressive and intimidating experience. Funny to think that she and Cherry might have walked past each other without knowing it.

But it was not the *Triumph* that she'd seen in port in Dio. It had been another, smaller ship.

"What was the *Triumph* doing in Dio?" she asked, hoping she sounded innocent, while the harbormaster made a call on her shell.

"It wasn't," Cherry said. "I was on secondment to another ship, the *Raptor*. They wouldn't send the *Triumph* to a place like that."

Annalie nodded and said nothing more.

The harbormaster returned. "I have notified the Admiralty," she said. "They are sending someone straight away." She looked at Annalie. "Did you wish to make a complaint about what happened to you in Dio? I can contact the police."

"I really just want to try and call my family," Annalie said.

"But you should file a complaint with the authorities," the harbormaster said.

"All I need is access to a shell," Annalie said.

The harbormaster looked at Cherry. Cherry looked back at her non-committally.

"*Please*," Annalie said.

The harbormaster nodded and placed a shell on the counter.

Annalie called her own number. It was answered on the first ring.

"Hello?"

"Will, it's me."

"Annalie!" Will shouted. "Where are you? What's going on?"

"Listen to me, you mustn't go and meet those pirates. I got away from them—I escaped."

"Seriously? How?"

"Long story," Annalie said, aware that Cherry and the harbormaster were both listening. "I need you to come and get me."

"Where are you?"

"Gantua," Annalie said, and named the town.

"Good," Will said. "I never want to go back to Brundisi as long as I live."

"When do you think you can get here?" she asked.

"I'm not exactly sure," Will said. "But sit tight. We'll be there as soon as we can. Are you safe?"

"Pretty safe," Annalie said. "I'm with an Admiralty officer. We escaped together."

"*What?*" squeaked Will. "Is that a joke?"

"Nope. And his ship is coming to pick him up

too, so it'll be fun to see who gets here first," Annalie said, trying to sound light and cheery.

"Oh, man," Will said. "Okay. Whose shell is that? Can we call you back on it?"

"Probably not," Annalie said, still trying to sound cheerful. "I'll update you if anything changes."

"Okay," Will said. "We're coming."

He hung up.

"They're coming," Annalie said simply, and handed back the shell.

Courtesy of the harbormaster, arrangements were made so Cherry could access his creditstream. "Come on, I'll buy you breakfast," he said.

They wandered into town, looking for somewhere to eat. Annalie felt newly awkward with him now. While they'd been locked in the room together, she had been able to see him as just another traveler like herself, a boy discovering the world from the deck of a boat. But now, back on shore, the differences between them reasserted themselves. He was no longer a fellow prisoner; he was about to rejoin the enemy. And she knew that at any moment, someone might take a closer look at an Admiralty watchlist—the harbormaster, for instance—and realize who she really was.

They found a café and sat down together, breakfasting Gantuans looking at them curiously. "Looks like they don't see a lot of out-of-towners here," she said, wondering whether she should be making herself so conspicuous.

"Don't worry," Cherry said, misunderstanding her. "You're perfectly safe here. Gantua isn't Brundisi."

Their food came quickly, and although it was unfamiliar, it was excellent. After their days in captivity, they were both starving.

"I really am grateful to you," Cherry said when he'd satisfied the worst of his hunger. "It wouldn't have occurred to me to escape like that if you hadn't pushed me into it."

"I'm just glad it worked," Annalie said.

"I'm serious," Cherry said. "If I'd been there on my own, I would have just kept on waiting until someone came for me. I don't know how long I would've been stuck there. The Admiralty doesn't pay ransoms and it doesn't negotiate with kidnappers, so I don't know how I expected them to get me out."

"Send in the marines, all guns blazing?" Annalie said jokingly, although she knew it wasn't really a joke. "Anyway, I couldn't have done it without you either."

Cherry looked at her for a moment, as if he was about to say something, but eventually he just smiled. "I'll get the bill."

They stepped out into the sunshine with full stomachs. "We should probably head back to the harbormaster's office," Cherry said. "There's just one more place we need to go first. Come with me—I need your help with something."

A little reluctantly, she followed him into a shop that sold a jumble of wares of all kinds, including lots of shells, old and new. "Which one should I get?" he asked her, indicating the shells.

"I'm not really an expert," Annalie said.

The shopkeeper came over to give advice on the relative merits of the makes and models. Cherry chose one, and a chip to go with it.

They stepped out of the shop. "Here," he said, and handed her the shell, along with a modest handful of Gantuan money.

"What's this for?" Annalie asked, surprised.

"Call it a thank-you present." He paused. "Use the money. Get away from here. Tell your friends to find somewhere else to pick you up, somewhere I don't know about." He paused. "I know who you are, Annalie."

Annalie felt suddenly dizzy. "How long have you known?" she asked.

"I didn't really work it out until yesterday," Cherry said. "But I wondered from the start."

"Oh," Annalie said.

He looked at her anxiously. "You know as soon as I get back to my ship, I'm going to have to tell them about you."

"Do you really have to?"

"It's my duty," Cherry said. "So the less I know about your plans, the better."

Annalie felt a surge of gratitude to this surprising young man. He was letting her escape in the best way he knew how. "Thank you," she said.

She was about to turn and go when Cherry spoke again. "I don't know what the real story is with you and your father," he said, "but I think you'd be an asset to the Admiralty if you ever came back."

"They'd never have me," Annalie said incredulously, "even if I wanted to. Which I don't."

Cherry frowned, perplexed. "I don't know who you think we are," he said, "but we're the good guys. Really."

"Some of you are," Annalie said.

Cherry shook his head and smiled. "You should go."

"Thank you," Annalie said again, and then she turned and hurried away into the crowd.

Annalie did exactly what Cherry had suggested. She contacted the others, Essie did some research, and they arranged to meet on the far side of Gantua. Annalie would travel there by train.

Gantuan trains were long and slow-moving, with many classes of carriage strung along their length, from luxury at the front to boxcar at the back. Annalie had chosen somewhere more or less in the middle, which meant she had a seat to sit on, she didn't have to share her carriage with livestock, and there was no one cooking on the floor, although it was crowded and very noisy.

She curled up quietly in her seat, hoping not to attract too much attention, still stunned by what had just happened. Cherry had known or at least suspected who she was from the very beginning, but he hadn't betrayed her. He'd befriended her, helped her, and then, when he had the chance to capture her—something that would no doubt have given his career an enormous boost—he'd let her go.

She felt fairly sure he was going to tell his superiors about her; he'd made that clear enough. But he'd done his best to give her a fighting chance to get away. He'd tried to find a solution that would help her while still allowing him to do his duty. She was charmed by the thought that he wanted to do his duty. He seemed the polar opposite of Beckett and his men.

She remembered a conversation she'd had once with Essie about the Admiralty and what they stood for. Essie had grown up believing the Admiralty were a band of heroes who sailed the world, righting wrongs and protecting the weak, and she'd been very upset when Annalie suggested that perhaps there was another, darker side to the Admiralty's power. Annalie hadn't grown up hating the Admiralty, although she had picked up Spinner's ambivalence about them. Her dislike and mistrust of them had really only begun when she met Beckett. He seemed like the living embodiment of everything that was frightening and hateful about the Admiralty: he was dangerous and manipulative, vindictive and violent, ruthless toward anyone he saw as an enemy. He seemed to have the freedom to sail the oceans of the world, pursuing his vendettas, and there was nothing that anyone could do about it.

But Cherry was different. Cherry seemed to represent that other Admiralty, the one Essie believed in.

He'd joined because he truly believed in their mission, and in his first year at sea, he really seemed to think he was making a difference.

In a way, she hoped he was right. It would be comforting to believe in *his* Admiralty.

But what was the point in her believing in it? She had cut herself off from all that when she ran away. After everything that had happened, there could be no going back, even if she wanted to. She was a traitor's daughter. There was no way back to her old home, her old life. The best she could hope for now was to be reunited with Spinner and find a new place to hide. It was a slightly depressing thought. Could they build new lives for themselves if they had to stay in the shadows forever, always afraid that Beckett might come after them?

For she knew that Beckett would never stop. He would never be appeased. Charges of treachery were not something that would simply go away. They would always be hanging over their heads now, forever.

The train rattled its way across Gantua, stopping many, many, many times. Annalie dozed, woke, watched the landscape slip by. The journey was a long one, but at last the noisy announcement system called out the name of her station, the train eased to the platform, and she stepped out into hot, dusty daylight on the far side of Gantua. From there, it was a long and thirsty walk down to the port, where the

Sunfish lay at anchor, waiting for her.

Will came in the dinghy to fetch her. She threw her arms around his neck, immensely relieved to see him.

"Good work getting away," he said.

"Same to you," Annalie said. "You still haven't told me how you guys got away from the pirates."

"We had help," Will said.

They zoomed back toward the *Sunfish*. Annalie took the shell Cherry had given her from her pocket and threw it overboard, in case they had some way of tracking it.

"So is everybody all right?" she shouted over the motor.

"Yes," Will shouted back. "There has been *one* new development though."

"What's that?" Annalie asked.

They reached the *Sunfish*. Annalie clambered up, noting it now had a bullet hole in its hull, as Will tied the dinghy up securely.

The others were waiting for her on deck. Essie ran to throw her arms around her. Annalie hugged her friend, tears of relief springing to her eyes now that she was finally home. She turned to look at Pod—and saw, to her shock, a strange girl standing beside him.

She was younger than the rest of them, maybe only ten or eleven, with Pod's thin build and her hair cropped short. She was dressed in Essie's sparkly jeans and top, and she watched Annalie's arrival with the wariness of a small wild animal.

"Annalie," Pod said, "meet my sister, Blossom."

Blue Water Duchess

"But what does that mean? Your dad will see what he can do?" Will asked.

Will, Pod, and Essie were anchored in the bay of Doria. Essie had triumphantly shown the boys the message she'd received from her father. Will was less impressed than she'd expected.

"It means he's going to try and get the money for us. We can save Annalie!" Essie said. "C'mon, give me some credit here!"

"Okay, that is good news," Will said grudgingly. "But how long is it going to take? You heard those pirates. They're not going to wait forever."

"Hello?" Essie said. "It's a hundred thousand creds. He can't just fish it out of the back of the couch, you know! It's going to take a bit of time, and if the pirates can't recognize that, they're idiots."

"That's what you're going to tell them, is it?" Will said.

"I'll tell them that if they're willing to be patient just a little bit longer, it'll be worth their while," Essie said. "And I'll make them believe it."

Will turned to Pod. "What do you think?"

But Pod wasn't paying attention. He was looking at the wide opening of Doria harbor, where a vast white shape had appeared and was moving in slow and stately fashion into the bay. A horn boomed out to announce its presence. "Pod?" Will said again.

Pod turned to them, trembling with excitement. "That writing—can you read what it says?"

"You mean the name of the cruise ship?" Will said.

Essie read it for him. "It's the *Blue Water Duchess*."

Pod let out a cry of joy. "That's the one!"

Essie twigged. "Your sister's boat?"

"Yes! *Duchess*! That's the one! We have to go there—now!"

"Wait—what?" Will said.

Pod looked at him impatiently. "My sister was on the *Blue Water Duchess*. I have to find her and get her back."

"What, now?" Will said.

"Yes, now!" Pod said. "This is my chance!"

"But what about Annalie?" Will said.

"We can't do anything until we hear from my dad," Essie said. "Why shouldn't he go?"

"Because we need to be ready," Will said. "As soon as we know the money's there, we've got to go, like, immediately! Annalie and the pirates are in Dio. We're here in Doria. They're calling us at 5 with further instructions, and you know there's no way we can get back to Brundisi in time, even if we start sailing right now."

"Yes, but we can't leave anyway, not until we've got the money sorted out," Essie argued. "The links are good here. If the pirates want cash, we'll be able to get it here. Why shouldn't Pod go to look for his sister, since we have to wait here anyway?"

"But what if something goes wrong?" Will said. "What if we have to go get her in a hurry, and *he's* off running around a cruise ship?" Will turned to Pod. "You don't even know she's on it anymore."

"That's why I have to go!" Pod said. "I have to find out!"

"They threatened to start cutting bits off my sister!" Will said.

"They're not going to do that!"

"You don't know that!"

For a moment, the two of them glared at each other.

"I might not get another chance," Pod said. "It has to be now. I've come halfway around the world to help you find your dad. Now, I need to find my sister. If you've got to leave without me, leave without me. But I'm going."

Pod turned resolutely and went to untie the dinghy.

Will watched him go, simmering with frustration. "You'd better bring that back!" he shouted as Pod started the engine and drove away.

The two of them watched in silence for a moment as Pod puttered off toward the shore. Then Essie turned to Will, frowning. "It's the only thing he wants in the whole wide world," she said.

"I know," Will said crossly, because he *did* understand. "Did it have to be now?"

It took a long time for the *Blue Water Duchess* to traverse the bay and arrive at the deep-water dock purpose-built for giant cruise ships. Tugs guided her in, and then as soon as the great ropes had lashed her securely to the shore, hordes of vessels and vehicles came swarming up to begin the enormous task of servicing the ship while the holidaymakers were disgorged into town.

Pod's plan was simple enough: he would pretend to be a tourist. It had got him and Essie aboard the *Blue Water Princess*. There was no reason it wouldn't work again. Impatiently, he watched the waves of cruisers as they came off the boat and fought their way through hordes of eager touts offering services, taxis, and trinkets. *Just act like you deserve to be there*, he reminded himself. He walked up to a uniformed steward guarding one of the gangways and tried to sound rich. "Hi. I left my shell in my room. Can I just go back and get it?"

The steward gave him one look and said, "You're not a passenger."

Pod glanced down at himself. He never thought much about clothes, and now, too late, he realized he looked more like a beggar than a tourist. Last time, he'd disguised himself in a souvenir t-shirt. He knew if Essie was here now she would have tried to brazen it out. But he didn't have her confidence.

"Go on, hop it, before I call the police," the steward said.

Temporarily defeated, Pod slunk away.

But he didn't go far. He found a good vantage point where he could watch the boat while he thought about what to do next. He couldn't walk on as a passenger. But could he try to sneak aboard as a crewman? He watched the boat's operations and saw that there were surprisingly few people other than passengers coming or going, or even visible on board the ship. Stewards controlled the gangways, but where were all the other staff? The maids and the maintenance men, the hands and the sailors?

He turned his attention to the goods being loaded onto and offloaded from the ship. Huge pallets were lined up on the dock ready to be loaded; a claw-like thing on a mighty mechanical arm lifted them up one by one and loaded them into a bay at the rear of the ship. Pod watched as the arm turned and lowered, grabbed and lifted. The whole process seemed smooth and efficient and was conducted without much intervention from actual people.

This, he decided, was his way in.

He stole out from his hiding place and crept toward the pallets. Most of them consisted of boxes of various sizes, packed in tight and swaddled with layers and layers of wrapping. There was no room on most of the pallets to squeeze in with the load. Then, at the far end of a row, he found what he was looking for: laundry, baled and tied. Wielding his pocket knife, he made a little slit in the wrapping, cut the twine holding one of the bales of laundry together, and pulled out enough towels to make a space for himself. Then he crept into the little gap he'd made, pulled the towels around himself, and waited.

The smell of laundry powder was overwhelming, and the smothering weight of all that fabric pressing in upon him from every side started a flutter of panic inside him. *Just breathe*, he told himself. *Think about Blossom.*

He hadn't seen his sister for two years. He wondered, as he often did, how she might have changed. She had been a sweet-natured girl when they were together, silly and funny when they were among friends, although silent and fearful when their masters were around. He had made her a doll out of sticks once, a poor enough thing, but she loved it. It was lost when they were moved from the failed farm to the hulk; she'd been devastated by the loss. She would be too old for dolls now, he guessed. He hoped life hadn't been too hard for her on the cruise ship. Boring, probably, with long hours. But not dangerous or frightening. At least he hoped not.

Suddenly, his pallet lurched. The towels against him bulged inwards as the claw gripped them and he had to squeeze sideways to avoid being squished. Then the pallet lifted into the air, leaving Pod's stomach behind. He felt an agony of fear at the unnatural sensation of floating free from the ground; then the pallet was descending. It landed with precision—barely a bump—and Pod let out his breath, grateful to have landed without mishap.

He peeped out carefully from his screen of towels. He was in a huge hold stacked with pallets; now, at last, he could see staff. People moved about, checking lists and ripping open wrappings, moving supplies with hand trolleys. These people all wore uniforms, several different ones. If he was going to move about the ship unseen, he would have to get hold of one.

Footsteps approached; he pulled his head back in behind the towels in the nick of time as someone walked right past him, but fortunately didn't stop.

When all was quiet again, he looked out. There was more laundry in some of the pallets nearby—some of it was sheets, but one contained bales of uniforms. He grabbed a jacket; he did not have time to look for pants. He pulled it on and hurried out of the hold.

On a cruise ship, the nicest parts of the ship were on the outside, where there was sunlight and a view. All the working parts of the ship were tucked away on the inside, where the light never reached. The *Blue Water Duchess* was a floating island ten storeys high, and her service areas were correspondingly vast. Pod wandered for a time, trying to get his bearings. This turned out to be a little easier than it seemed at first; the crew on a ship like this spoke many languages, and like Pod, many of them couldn't read. So while there were written signs on the service corridors, they were mostly accompanied by symbols which made it easy to sort out the engines from the plumbing, the kitchens from the laundry, and maintenance from housekeeping. Blossom had been taken on as a maid; if she was still working in the same division, housekeeping was where he was most likely to find her.

He followed the symbols along metal service corridors and up and down clanging stairwells, all lit by the same harsh, unfriendly greenish light. No one really stopped to look at him as they went by; he guessed they all had something to do, and on a boat this large you might never get to know all the crew. The first time he saw a maid coming toward him, he stopped her and said, "Excuse me, I'm looking for Blossom. You seen her?" The maid stared at him blankly, then shook her head and hurried away. He kept going, looking into service bays and storage cupboards and waiting rooms and dormitories, descending and descending through endless levels. He saw no one he recognized, and no one seemed to know Blossom. He descended another level and arrived in a wide corridor. Ahead of him, a maid was slowly pushing a trolley laden with cleaning supplies.

"Excuse me," he began, but before she even turned around he felt a blaze of recognition, and he said, "Blossom?"

She turned and her face brightened with joy, then she ran and threw her arms around him.

Blossom

Blossom looked both the same and different. The last time Pod had seen her, she'd still had a little girl's face; now, she looked even older than Essie and Annalie, although he knew she was younger than they were. She was wearing make-up, which made her look older than she was, and she was developing an adult's bone structure. But more than that, the person behind her eyes was not a child anymore. She was delighted to see him now, laughing and happy, but in the split-second before she recognized him, he'd seen a darkness that disturbed him.

"Pod!" she cried. "What are you doing here?"

"I got my freedom," Pod said. "I've come to get you out of here."

For a moment, Blossom stared at him blankly. Then she gave a startled, disbelieving laugh. "You messing with me?" she asked.

"Nope," Pod said. "I'm free, and I've come to rescue you."

"You're messing," Blossom said again.

"I'm really not," Pod said. "So, how do we get out of here?"

"It's impossible."

Pod felt a cold feeling steal through him. "There must be a way."

"If there was," Blossom said, "we'd *all* be out of here."

She explained that whenever the boat was in port, the crew was locked down to prevent them from escaping. All the access doors that connected the service areas to the passenger areas were kept locked; only the most senior crew members were allowed out at these times.

"What happens if there's a fire?" Pod asked.

"We put it out," Blossom said.

"They wouldn't even unlock the doors if there was a fire?"

"Nope."

"I don't suppose you could talk someone into letting you through the doors?" Pod suggested.

Blossom laughed. "Me? No." She looked at him. "How'd you get in here, anyway?"

Pod explained about the claw and the bay filled with pallets. Blossom pulled a face. "Once they finish loading the supplies, they close the hatch," she said. "It'll be closed now."

Pod pondered some more. "What about all the stuff they take off the ship?" he asked. "If there's clean laundry coming aboard, there must be dirty laundry somewhere too, right?"

"There is," Blossom said, "but they lock it up so you can't get at it."

"Are you sure?" Pod asked.

"People used to sneak out in the dirty laundry," Blossom said. "So they made it impossible."

"Isn't there *any* way off this boat?"

"Well, I did hear one thing—" Blossom stopped.

"Well? What did you hear?"

"They say someone got out in the garbage," Blossom said.

"What do they do with the garbage?" Pod asked. The crew of the pirate ship he'd been on and the slave hulk before it had simply thrown all their rubbish overboard, although neither would have done it in port.

"I heard there's a barge," Blossom said. "They open a hatch and all the rubbish from the boat plops out onto the barge and they take it away. I heard that once someone dropped themselves down the garbage chute and escaped that way. But I also heard someone drowned in the garbage because there was so much of it."

"Maybe that's it," Pod said. "Maybe that's our way out."

A look of dark, antic mischief crept over Blossom's face. "Through the garbage chute? You ever smelled one of those things? It's like all the worst smells in the world got together in one place."

"If it's our only option ..." Pod said.

Blossom grinned wickedly. "Okay then. But I need to get some things first."

She abandoned her trolley and scampered off down the corridor, Pod chasing after her. She led him to a dormitory where many bunks were packed in tightly together, currently unoccupied as all the maids were working. The narrow bunks all had the same cheap bedlinen on them, but many of them were personalized with pictures and mementoes, scraps of colored fabric, personal treasures. Blossom's bunk was largely unadorned. She stripped the pillowcase off the one pillow, then glanced furtively around her and lifted up the mattress. She did not give Pod a chance to see what was under there; whatever she had hidden, she quickly swept it into the pillowcase and twisted it tightly closed. "Let's go," she said.

She led him through another maze of corridors, heading steadily down. After a while, a nasty smell reached him. It was a heavy, organic sort of smell that gradually grew more nauseating and intense. Blossom turned and grinned at him. "See?" she said.

She turned a corner, then quickly pulled back.

"What is it?" asked Pod.

"There are guards on the door."

Pod stood there in silence for a moment, thinking. "I've got an idea," he said. "Can you act upset?"

"Huh?"

"Try to look like you're in fear for your life."

He hurried around the corner, Blossom following, and rushed up to the guards on the garbage bay door.

"Hey, listen, we're in serious trouble," Pod said. "My sister accidentally put a passenger's jewelry in the garbage when she was cleaning up the room. It's got to be in here somewhere, and we've got to get it back before the passenger realizes it's missing."

The two guards stared at him. "Do you mean you want to go *in there*?" the taller one asked.

"You know that's not allowed," said the shorter one.

Blossom suddenly erupted. "Oh, please," she wailed. "I already signed the room off, so if the passenger reports me, I'll be in so much trouble!"

The guards exchanged looks. "It's strictly forbidden," the tall one said.

"We're due for clearance any minute," the short one said.

"If they think I stole the jewelry, it's all over for me," Blossom wailed, wringing her hands. "Please."

Pod thought she was rather overdoing it, but the guards seemed taken in.

"You don't know what it's like in there," the tall guard said. "You'll never find it."

"At least let us try," Pod said. "Please?"

The guards looked at each other again, clearly considering it. "But what about the drop?" the short one murmured.

The tall one screwed up his face, then said, "You can have five minutes. Then you got to be out."

"And never breathe a word of this to anyone," the short one added.

"Of course not," Blossom said eagerly. "Thank you!"

"Be quick," the tall one said.

The two of them unbolted the doors and cranked them open just enough to let Pod and Blossom slip through. They'd thought the smell was bad before, but when the doors cracked apart for the first time and the smell of the garbage hold breathed out over

them, Pod felt like he was going to be sick. The reek
was so foul and potent it could burn metal.

"Five minutes," the guard warned.

They stepped inside the hold.

The doors clanged shut.

They were trapped.

The hatch

It was perfectly dark inside.

Luckily for them both, Blossom carried a flashlight in the pocket of her uniform, and she switched this on now. Garbage, loose and in bags, towered all around them in vast, slimy heaps. Things moved and scuttled around them, scampering away in the dark.

"Rats," Pod said.

"I hate rats," Blossom said.

For a moment they both stood there, rigid with fear and disgust. The smell was overwhelming.

"Now what?" Blossom said.

"I guess we try and find the hatch," Pod said.

Together they began to climb over the mountains of garbage. It was a horrible experience. Bags squelched and slithered and sometimes split under their hands and feet, so they went sprawling into old, spoiled food and used tissues and bits of hair and all kinds of disgustingness. Rats squeaked at them and ran about. They kept hearing a slithering sound which grew louder and louder, followed by a brief period of silence and then a thump as garbage dropped down the chutes. Once, a bag dropped down right between them, almost taking them out, and then burst in a shower of rancid stink.

They heard a clang; the doors had opened. "Oi!" came the tall guard's voice. "Five minutes are up! You'd better get back here!"

"We're still looking!" Pod shouted. "Just one minute more!" He turned to Blossom. "Keep moving," he murmured. "Hurry."

The guards were not in a mood to be patient. "Time's up!" the guard shouted. "You got to get out of there! It's dangerous!"

"Where do you reckon the hatch is?" Pod asked Blossom. He ran the flashlight beam over the distant wall of the hold, but it wasn't strong enough to pick out any detail. Another load came slipping and slithering down a chute.

"We're going to have to lock the door!" the short guard shouted. "You'll be locked in there!"

After a moment, they heard the clank and grind of the door being closed and bolted.

"This is it," Pod gulped. "No going back now."

"What do you think it's going to be? Get free? Or drown?"

Pod looked at Blossom, surprised. In the weak glow of the flashlight, she didn't look frightened at all. If anything, she looked excited.

An alert sounded, a loud, terrifying honking sound. The rats bolted, all traveling in the same direction, scurrying up the rubbish and away. Far across the hold they saw a hatch slide up. "Quick," Pod said, "let's try and get to it!" Just as they were renewing their efforts to scramble across the garbage, they heard a new sound. An engine started up. There was a clank and a clunk, and then the wall behind them began to move.

They climbed frantically across the garbage, trying to stay ahead of the wall as it moved inexorably across the hold, pushing all the garbage toward the open hatch. If they got caught up in that growing wall of filth, they could be crushed and smothered under the weight of it. They scrambled forward, panic making them clumsy, sinking into the garbage. The open air and the smell of the sea was tantalisingly close, but the garbage was mounding up behind them like a tsunami. Blossom slipped and started to disappear under the garbage. Pod reached out and pulled her free, and they dragged themselves the last few feet toward the hatch.

"It's too far!" Blossom cried, looking down at the drop to the garbage barge below them. It was easily thirty feet down.

Pod looked behind them; the wall of garbage was getting bigger and bigger, and it would collapse on them at any moment. "Jump!" he cried, and yanked her.

They jumped—

They fell through the air—

They landed on soft bags of rubbish which burst wetly beneath them, breaking their fall.

Pod grabbed Blossom as soon as they'd landed and they rolled out of the drop zone, creeping to the edge of the huge barge as the sliding pile of garbage grew to a torrent.

"Someone's going to see us for sure," Pod said.

"We should hide."

They found some broken bags and draped them over their heads, peering out through the gaps. Blossom looked at Pod from her dark cocoon of plastic like a bright-eyed creature looking out of its burrow. "Now what?"

"I don't know," Pod said. "Let me think."

The garbage chute was on the ocean side of the *Blue Water Duchess*, but even so, the dock was probably only fifty yards away. If either of them knew how to swim, they could have simply swum ashore. But that wasn't an option. He couldn't see anything on the barge that they could steal to help them float ashore, and there was always the risk that someone from the *Blue Water Duchess* might spot them and have them arrested and taken back to the ship.

He turned to look at the bridge of the barge. The crew were in there, but no one seemed to be looking in their direction. He hoped that meant no one had seen them drop.

Above them, they heard a new sound: the outer hatch on the *Blue Water Princess* was closing. Radio voices scratched and rumbled from the bridge. The idling engines began to spin. The barge was leaving.

"Where does this go?" Blossom said.

"I don't know," Pod said. "We'll just stay on it till we're clear of the ship. Then we'll get off."

"Okay," Blossom said. "How?"

But he didn't yet have an answer to that.

The barge pulled away from the ship. Pod hoped it would motor somewhere along the side of the harbor, but to his dismay, it turned and headed straight out toward the mouth. Wherever the barge dumped its load, it wasn't anywhere nearby. He hoped the garbage men didn't just take it all out to sea and dump it there.

"I think we need to get off this thing," he said. "And soon."

He looked around, hoping for inspiration. The barge was moving at quite a clip, and they were headed for deep water, the land receding rapidly into the distance. They had no hope of swimming for shore. What if they jumped overboard near another boat and signaled for rescue? But there were no other boats berthed nearby. They were traveling up a wide shipping channel; it was not a place for swimmers to be, especially when they were swimmers who couldn't swim. Big ships could run them down without ever seeing them.

He heard a shout. He turned; a crewman had appeared from the bridge. They'd been seen. The crewman was clambering along a catwalk, moving purposefully toward them.

"They'll make us go back!" Blossom hissed.

Desperately, Pod looked around for something, anything, that would help them escape.

A marker buoy floated not too far off, marking the edge of the shipping lane. It wasn't much, but it was afloat. "Jump!" he said in desperation. "Make for that thing!"

"You know I can't swim!" Blossom cried.

"Jump!" Pod shouted.

He leaped, and after a moment, Blossom leaped

after him. He scrabbled in the water, paddling frantically until his fingers brushed something solid. He grabbed for it—it was the rope holding the buoy in place—and held on, breathing a sigh of relief, but then Blossom landed on him, a clambering, panicking, wild thing, pushing his head under as she struggled to stay on the surface. Pod almost lost his grip on the rope as he tried to right himself, Blossom fighting him in her fear.

"Grab on to the buoy!" he spluttered. She floundered and fought until she managed to get a hand onto the buoy, then wrapped her arms around it, and only then did she relinquish her grip on him.

Pod turned to see what the barge was doing. To his relief, it was moving on, although the crewman was still standing there watching them.

Pod gave him a half-hearted wave, not sure what else to do. The crewman crinkled his brow, shaking his head, but made no further move toward them. The barge continued on its way.

Pod watched it until he was sure it was not coming back for them, then tried to work out what to do next. He scanned the harbor and, to his huge relief, spotted the *Sunfish* lying at anchor. It was still a long way away, but they were at least on the right side of the shipping channel. Now all he had to do was get there.

"I wish this thing had a motor," Blossom said.

That gave Pod an idea. "We've got legs," he said.

Using his pocket knife, he cut the rope holding the buoy in place, turned it toward the distant shape of the *Sunfish*, and began to kick.

It was not easy and the buoy did not steer very straight, but slowly and patiently, Pod kicked the two of them and their buoy toward the boat. Just as he was thinking he could not go on much longer, something splashed near him.

It was a life preserver. He looked up and saw a wonderful sight: Will standing on the deck, holding the other end of the rope.

"Who wants to go first?" Will asked.

The Lucky Lady

Pod scrambled onto the deck. Blossom had climbed up ahead of him and was standing on the deck of the *Sunfish*, looking around her. She turned to him and said, "This boat is really *small*."

"No it isn't," Pod said, embarrassed, in case Will had taken it as a slight.

"It is if you compare it to a cruise ship," Will said, unconcerned. "But it's big enough for us. I'm Will."

"I'm Essie," said Essie, smiling at Blossom encouragingly. "I'm so excited to meet you!"

Blossom blinked at them both uncertainly. "Hi," she said.

"Pod stinks!" Graham rasped.

Blossom's eyes widened. "Is that a talking bird? What else can it say?"

Graham ruffled his feathers. "Anything it wants," he said haughtily.

"No offense, but you do reek," Will said. "What happened?"

"Maybe we should have a shower," Pod said, "and then we can tell you the whole story."

He took Blossom down to the heads and turned

the shower on. "Do you want to go first?" he asked.

"Sure," Blossom said. She shucked off her clothes and stepped under the water. After a minute or two she opened her eyes again and noticed Essie's shampoo and conditioner. "Can I use these?" she asked.

"I guess," Pod said.

She mixed them both together and lathered herself with them all over, making fragrant clouds of bubbles. When she was about to pour out a second round—which would have emptied the bottles—Pod called time. "I think you're clean enough now," he said.

Reluctantly Blossom got out of the water and Pod stepped in, washing the garbage stink out of his hair and from under his fingernails until he was clean again. Then he quickly rinsed his clothes out too.

When he stepped out of the shower, Blossom was still standing there wrapped in a towel. "I'm not putting *that* thing on ever again," she said, prodding her discarded uniform with her toe.

"Maybe Essie has something you could borrow," Pod said.

He called up the stairs for Essie; moments later she appeared. "Of course you can borrow something," she said.

She took Blossom into the cabin she shared with Annalie. Neither of them had brought a lot of clothes with them, but what they did have was stashed in a locker. She began looking for something that might fit Blossom, who was lean and lanky like Pod, but Blossom had already seen what she wanted.

"What about these?" she asked excitedly.

She pulled out the sparkly jeans and top Essie had been wearing the night she and Annalie ran away from school. Essie hadn't worn them for a while—the sequins made her feel too conspicuous, and the jeans had been a bit hot for the Moon Islands—but it *had* been one of her favorite outfits once, and besides, the jeans were designer, and expensive. "Oh—" she said.

But then she saw the look of longing on Blossom's face, and thought about how *she'd* feel if she was a recently freed slave, and she said, "Well, okay. Sure."

Blossom looked gleeful. The towel dropped to the ground. She began to get dressed. Essie left her to it.

On her way out, she told Pod, "We got the ransom money. We need to go back to Brundisi to get Annalie. You'd better tell Blossom we're leaving."

"Okay," Pod said. He got an uneasy feeling as he wondered how to break this news to his sister.

Soon Blossom appeared, ready to show herself off. "How do I look?"

"Fancy," he said.

She drew closer and lowered her voice, even though the others were up on deck and could not hear them. "Those people," she said. "Who are they?"

"I told you," Pod said. "They're my friends."

"But did they buy you or what?"

"Of course not!" Pod said. "Actually, they rescued me. My last master was a pirate, and he threw me overboard. These guys found me in the middle of the ocean."

"Serious?" Blossom said.

"Serious," Pod said.

"So now you work for them?"

"We all work together."

Blossom's brow knitted. It still wasn't quite making sense to her. "So who's *their* master? Whose boat is this?"

"It belongs to Will and Annalie's dad. He's missing, and we're looking for him."

"I thought the girl's name was Essie?"

"It is. You haven't met Annalie yet. She's Will's twin sister."

"And where is she?"

"She was kidnapped by pirates."

Blossom's eyes narrowed. "Pirates?"

Pod could see he had some explaining to do. Briefly he told her the story of Spinner and the search for the scientists, their ill-fated trip to Brundisi, and the kidnapping of Annalie. "Now we're going back for her. But it's all going to be fine, I promise."

"Are they rich?" she asked eagerly.

"No!" Pod said.

"Then why did the pirates kidnap her?"

"I don't know! All I know is we have to go and get her back."

"Wait—we?"

"Yeah," Pod said.

"You're going back to Brundisi? Are you serious?"

"We have to get her back," Pod said.

"They're going to kill her," Blossom said. "Then they'll take the money, take the boat, and kill you."

"No they're not," Pod said, although this scenario had certainly occurred to him.

"You can't go to Brundisi," Blossom said. "It's too dangerous. She's his sister, let *him* go."

"We're all going," Pod said. "We're a team."

"*I'm* not going," Blossom said.

"I can't leave you behind," Pod said.

"Of course not!" Blossom said. "You're staying right here with me. Hey, you got papers? How hard d'you think it would be to get a job here?"

"I can't stay here with you," Pod said. "I have to go with the others and get Annalie. They're counting on me."

For a long, terrible moment, Blossom stared at him, her eyes growing huge and wide. "But—you came to rescue *me*."

"I know I did. And now I'm taking you with me."

"To be killed by pirates?" She was horrified.

"It's going to be all right, I promise!" Pod said helplessly.

Blossom's eyes were bright with tears. "Why take me off the ship if you're just going to take me somewhere even worse?" she demanded.

Her look of betrayal pierced him. "I'm sorry," he said. "I guess I didn't really think it through. But ever since you went away on that first boat, I've been looking for you."

"You mean the *Blue Water Princess*?"

"Yes! One day we ran into the *Princess* and me and Essie snuck aboard. That's how I found out they'd moved you to the *Duchess*. And when I saw the *Duchess* was here, I couldn't believe my luck. It's like I was meant to find you."

Blossom's expression altered. "Do you think *she* made it happen?"

"She?" Pod was confused. For a moment he thought she meant Essie.

"*The Lucky Lady*," Blossom whispered.

Pod was surprised. In their first job together, they'd been part of a crew of young people who were sent down into flooded underwater places to search in the dark for salvage. The other kids believed that the world was ruled by sea gods, who controlled the oceans, and the Lucky Lady, who protected the people who ventured into the water. The Lucky Lady had miraculous powers and could save anyone if she chose to; under her protection, no disaster could touch you. But the Lucky Lady was capricious and her whims were mysterious; her favor could vanish as easily as it was given. As a child, he'd believed in the Lucky Lady with the ferocity of someone who needed to believe there was something in the world that could keep him safe. Now he was not so sure, but the idea of her still appealed.

"I don't know," Pod said cautiously. "Maybe she did. All I know is, this was my chance, and it might be the only one I ever get. I had to come and find you. Even though the timing isn't great."

Blossom shot him a sidelong glance, still rather accusing, but he hoped she might be gradually softening. "Timing's terrible," she said.

"I promise I'll do everything I can to keep you safe," Pod said. "And so will the others. They're amazing people. You'll see. They're the best friends I ever had in the world."

"Apart from me," she said.

"You're more than a friend. You're my sister," Pod said, and felt something wobble inside him.

"The only one you got," Blossom said, "and don't you forget it."

They were both silent for a moment.

"So," Pod said. "What do you think?"

She looked at him challengingly, her eyes as sharp and bright as the sequins on her top. "One: if you get me killed by pirates, I'm going to haunt you so bad it's not funny," she said. "And two: after we find this girl—and her dad—can we find somewhere to live?"

"Sure," Pod said.

"Can it be Violeta? I always wanted to go to Violeta."

"Okay," Pod said. He had never heard of Violeta and had no idea where it was. "Does that mean you'll come?"

Blossom shrugged, her old fearless self again. "Where else am I going to go?"

The end of the east

"So where's Blossom going to sleep now that Annalie's back?" Will asked.

The *Sunfish* had only two cabins; before Blossom's arrival, the girls had shared one and the boys had shared the other. The cushions on the benches in the saloon could be removed to make a bed on the floor, but who would take the bed on the floor?

"Let Blossom sleep on the floor," Will said. "Last in, last to a bed."

"You can't make her sleep on the floor," Essie protested.

"I'll sleep on the floor," Pod said. "I don't mind."

"But then where will Blossom sleep?" Essie asked.

"She can share with Essie and I'll share with Will," Annalie suggested.

Neither Will nor Essie was thrilled by this idea.

"Ask *her* where she wants to sleep!" Graham said.

Pod turned to Blossom. "Blossom, who do you want to share with?"

Blossom's answer came instantly. "No one."

"But do you mind sleeping on the floor?" Annalie asked.

"Where?"

They looked around. Annalie pointed out a spot that was more or less out of the way, although floor space was not exactly at a premium. "How about here? We could put a curtain up for privacy at night, and we could empty a locker for you so you could have somewhere to put your stuff. We'd have to pack it away during the day though."

"Okay," Blossom said.

"Are you sure that's what you want?" Pod asked, slightly disappointed that she didn't want to share a cabin with him.

"Yes," Blossom said decisively.

So that question was settled.

They spent a single day in the little Gantuan port town where they'd come to collect Annalie. They had seen no sign of Beckett's ship, but they knew it could not be far away; they had to hope no one had spotted Annalie or the *Sunfish* and reported them to the Admiralty. But they could not sail immediately for Sundia; the journey ahead of them would be long and there would be no help along the way, so they had to make sure they were fully provisioned before they set sail again.

Sundia was located in the Outer Ocean, one of the largest and emptiest oceans in the world. It stretched from the east of the Brundisan continent, extending a third of the way around the globe until it struck the west coast of Dux. The Outer Ocean was huge and empty, with only a few small island groupings in the north and Sundia grandly isolated in the south. It was famous for having wild and terrifying weather, especially in the south, where huge winds circled the globe with nothing much to slow them down, whipping up giant waves and tempests that lasted for days, or so the story went.

They didn't expect to encounter much traffic on the way to Sundia. There was little reason to cross the Outer Ocean unless you were going to Sundia, and since their borders were closed, few people made the attempt. The Admiralty patrolled the edges of the Outer Ocean, on both the Duxan and Gantuan sides, but they did not patrol the Ocean itself. It was too big, too empty; there was little in the way of shipping to protect, no pirate bases, no island nations. Just water. Lots and lots and lots of rough, stormy water.

No wonder early sailors had called it the Desert Ocean: sailing into it was like sailing into a desert, where there was no land, no people, no supplies, no help. Many ships had vanished there. It was this uncomfortable fact that had once given the Outer Ocean its other name—the Ocean of Monsters—and had given rise to stories about terrible beasts that lived in it: enormous sea monsters who rammed ships with their armored heads and sank them, or huge slimy things with tentacles that wrapped their suckery arms around boats and dragged them down to the depths.

Modern exploration had made the ocean more navigable, less terrifying, banishing the tales of ship-breaking monsters to the realms of fantasy; and the discovery of Sundia—a strange paradise, vast and abundant, isolated from the rest of the world—had transformed it from a place of death to a place of possibility. But even so, the crew of the *Sunfish* knew they were sailing into some of the most remote territory they had yet encountered. And Sundia itself was almost as much of an unknown.

"I did see a cool vid once about the Sundians," Essie said. "They were originally from the Moon Islands, and they made boats out of reeds and just sailed around the world until they got to Sundia. And once they got there, they didn't see anyone else for like a thousand years—or five thousand years, I don't remember exactly—and then explorers from the north came, and it all got quite bad, and there was some kind of war ... Anyway, the Sundians believe in sea gods, lots of different sea gods, and when the Flood happened, they thought it was the gods' judgment, and that's when they stopped letting foreigners in."

Blossom's ears pricked up at the mention of the sea gods. "They know about the sea gods there?"

"I think they invented them," Essie said.

"So what do you know about their defenses?" Will said. "Why is it so hard to get in there?"

"I don't know," Essie said. "I'll see what I can find out."

While Pod and Will went ashore for supplies, Essie loaded all the information she could find about Sundia onto her shell. She found old tourist guides and maps, information about Sundian politics and religion, and infrequent news reports that emerged from the isolated nation. When the others returned, she gave them some of the highlights.

"The Supreme Leader of the Sundians says the sea gods will protect their shores against foreign aggressors," Essie read.

"Does he say how they do that?" Will asked.

"Not really," Essie said.

"If they've only got made-up gods looking after them, this might be easier than we thought," Will said.

"Don't say that!" Blossom snapped.

"Say what?" Will said, genuinely confused.

"That they're made up! You'll make them angry!"

Will looked at her for a moment in disbelief, then said: "Personally, I'm more worried about defenses I can see, like patrol boats and guns, but okay. Sorry, sea gods."

Blossom did not look pacified, but she said nothing more.

They began their long journey south, spending every quiet moment working on their plans.

Sola Prentice, the last of the scientists, lived in a place called the International Bio-Archive and Research Cooperative—or the Ark, for short. It wasn't on any of the tourist maps, but it appeared on one very detailed pre-Flood government map. The Ark was the most remote place they'd tried to get to so far, even more remote than Sujana's little house in the mountains of Norlind. It was located in the vast arid desert that lay inland from Sundia's south-west coast, which was the most remote part of the remote island nation. The cities and old tourist attractions had been clustered around the north coast and down into the east; the south-west, for reasons they would soon discover, had never been particularly attractive to visitors.

"It looks like there's only one road in and out," Annalie said, studying the map. A line led from the dot that was the Ark to another dot on the coast.

"I'm not even sure it's a proper road," Essie said. "It's only a dotted line."

"And this map was made forty years ago," Will said. "Who knows what's there now?"

"If people are still living there, there must be some way to get there," Annalie said.

"We can't exactly rock up and ask them for a lift, though, can we?" Will said. "We're not even supposed to be there. We're going to have to find a way to get there under our own steam."

"It'll be a long walk," Annalie said.

"Through the desert," Essie added.

They all stared at the dotted line for a moment.

"Maybe we're overthinking it," Essie said. "We think Spinner's still there, right? We can just contact him, and he can get us picked up."

They all thought about the many times they'd tried to contact Spinner, and failed.

"I think we need a Plan B," Will said.

He spent a lot of time looking over the documents Essie had collected, studying the terrain, looking at pictures. Something he saw gave him an idea, and after that he spent all his spare hours up on deck, making something.

"What are you building?" Annalie asked.

"It's just an idea," Will said.

"What sort of idea?"

"You'll find out when it's done."

The only person who didn't have much to do was Blossom. Pod had hoped she'd look for some way to pitch in and help, as he did when he first joined the crew, but Blossom didn't seem to feel any need to work. She idled through the days, napping, dozing, staring into the water, chatting to anyone who was available, and teasing Graham. Sometimes she disappeared under the curtain they'd set up for her—if it hadn't been packed away for the day—and played quiet games on her own. They'd hear her voice murmuring away, but she got very cross if anyone tried to find out what she was doing. In some ways, she was ferociously protective of her privacy. Pod was very embarrassed by her refusal to help out and began nagging her, but it had absolutely no effect. She could not be shamed. Words and guilt bounced right off her.

"I'm sorry," he said to the others. "I don't know why she's being like this."

"Maybe she feels like she's done enough work for a while and she wants to have a bit of a holiday," Essie suggested.

"But she should help," Pod agonized. "It's not fair to everyone else."

"What would she help with?" Will said. "She doesn't know how to sail or fish or do anything useful."

"She could learn," Essie pointed out.

"Eventually she's going to get bored," Annalie

130

said. "Maybe we can find her something to do then."

But Blossom showed no sign of getting bored enough for that.

Despite all the dire reports they'd read about the Outer Ocean, its many dangers and its horrible weather, the first part of their journey was trouble-free, except for one thing. Things began to go missing.

First it was a seashell Annalie kept in her cabin. It wasn't valuable, but Spinner had given it to her, and she liked it. One day it was there, the next day it wasn't. Annalie thought it might have fallen on the floor, but a search of the cabin failed to turn it up. It seemed like one of those annoying things that happened: innocent. Accidental.

Next thing to go was a little mug shaped like a dog. It had been given to Will when he was a little boy, and because it was indestructible, it remained part of the galley crockery—until it wasn't.

Then Will discovered a spare reflector panel for the biggest solar cell was missing. This was a more serious problem; although the component was small, it was important, because if the panel failed and could not be replaced, it meant their biggest solar cell was out of action. Will knew for a fact that they had had a spare when they left Gantua; he'd checked it before they went on their last supply run. Now it too was missing from the locker where it was kept.

No one thought to connect these annoying absences until Essie's shell went missing. Essie turned the cabin inside out looking for it. Then she checked the boys' cabin and every locker in the saloon. The shell was

131

nowhere to be found. She asked everybody in turn if they'd seen it, even Graham. But no one had.

"What could have happened to it?" Essie asked, almost in tears. "It's nowhere!"

"It has to be somewhere," Will said. "There's nowhere it could have gone."

"Then why can't we find it?" Essie wailed.

"Something weird's going on," Will said. "These things going missing. The reflector. Your shell."

A thought occurred to him then, and it occurred to the rest of them at more or less the same time. Pod turned bright red. Then he went and stuck his head under Blossom's curtain. "Blossom, are you sure you don't know where Essie's shell is? It's very important that we find it."

Blossom looked back at him with an expression of consummate innocence. "No. I don't know where it is."

At that moment, all of them became convinced that Blossom had been stealing from them. And none of them had the faintest idea what to do about it.

Annalie beckoned to the others and moved them all upstairs.

Graham said what everybody was thinking. "Thief!"

"We don't *know* she is," Annalie said, striving for fairness.

"Easy enough to find out," Will said. "We go down there and see what she's hiding under that curtain."

"We can't!" Essie said.

"You're okay with letting her keep your shell?"

Essie was not. "We need to find a way to do it

without embarrassing her," she said. "We've got a long journey ahead of us."

"Screw that," Will said. "If she's stealing from us, she's got bigger problems than being embarrassed."

"Let me do it," Pod said. He was mortified by his sister's behavior. "I brought her on board. I'll fix this."

He went downstairs again, anger and embarrassment competing for the upper hand. How could she do this? To his friends? To *him*? Who had she become in the years they'd been apart? He didn't recognize the girl who'd returned from the cruise ship. And he had no idea how to handle her now.

Will would have gone in all guns blazing and started rifling through her things. But Pod had a feeling that such a thing, once done, would be hard to undo. So he kneeled down at the edge of the curtain and said, "Blossom? Can I come in?"

She peeped out at him like some bright-eyed, rather bitey creature peering from its burrow. "Why?"

"I need to talk to you."

Not taking no for an answer, he eased in under the curtain.

"You need to give it back," he said, trying to sound calm.

"I don't have it."

"Yes, you do."

She was silent for a moment, assessing him. Then she opened the locker that had been emptied for her and took out Essie's shell.

Inside, many objects had been carefully arranged on what he realized was the pillowcase she'd brought

133

with her from the *Blue Water Duchess*. He saw the dog mug, the solar reflector, and another shiny spare part they hadn't yet realized was missing. There were more things too, some of it cheap junk (a plastic jewel, a tiny notebook with a pink pen attached by a chain), some of it clearly very valuable (a personal electronic music player, an expensive-looking ring with real stones in it). He realized these must have been stolen from the cruise ship. Then he noticed there was a little girl's doll, with a bright mane of hair and huge blue-green eyes, a tiny waist and impossibly long legs, standing at the center of all these treasures. At once he understood what he was looking at: it was a shrine to the Lucky Lady.

"Where did you get all this stuff?" he asked.

"I found it."

"Really?"

"*Yes*," Blossom said savagely. "Rich people leave stuff behind all the time. They have so much, they don't even notice it's missing."

"You took this from the guests? Wouldn't you have gotten into big trouble for that?"

"Only if you got caught," Blossom said with a glint in her eye. "But I *didn't* steal it. I found it."

Pod didn't really believe her, but he suspected she half-believed it herself, or had said it to herself enough times that it had begun to seem true.

"What about these?" he said, pointing to the things she'd acquired on the boat. "Were these lost?"

Blossom made a sullen face, but said nothing.

"You can't steal their stuff," Pod said. "That's rule number one."

134

Blossom nodded, not meeting his eyes.

"I mean it. Not even little things. Not even if you think they'll never ever notice. Are you listening?"

"Yes!" Blossom said crossly.

"Do you promise?"

"*Yes!*"

Pod hoped he could believe her. "Okay," he said. "Can I take these?"

"They're offerings!" Blossom protested. "You can't take back an offering!"

"Which is worse," Pod countered, "taking back an offering, or giving the Lady something which isn't yours?"

While Blossom was still thinking about this, he scooped up the missing objects.

"Some people have *so much*, and other people have nothing," Blossom burst out bitterly. "It's not fair!"

"I'll tell you what's not fair," Pod said, beginning to lose his temper. "It's being here on their boat, eating their food, never lifting a finger to help, and then stealing from them."

"I never asked to come here," Blossom shot back.

"But you *are* here," Pod said, "and you can't *do* stuff like this. Not to my friends. Not to me."

Blossom looked at him defiantly, but her chin was starting to quiver. "You care more about them than you care about me."

"That's not true," Pod said.

"This is just like being back on the ship," Blossom said bitterly. "Someone's always taking your stuff away from you."

135

"It wasn't your stuff!" Pod said for what felt like the millionth time. Then he thought about what she'd just said. "Is that what used to happen on the ship? People would take your stuff?"

Blossom nodded. "Anything good you got, someone was always trying to take it away from you, unless you hid it real good." She paused. "Stealing was a big crime. Get caught stealing, they'd put you off the ship, send you to jail. Sometimes they did dorm searches in the middle of the night. Tore everything apart looking for stolen property."

"Did they find any?"

"Found all sorts of things. The other girls said security did it to take all our stuff for themselves. Sometimes people just did it for revenge—snitch on someone you didn't like, get them into trouble, get them sent off the boat."

"That's terrible," Pod said.

Blossom shrugged, then looked at him, defiance mixed with fear. "So what are you going to do to me?" she asked.

Pod was baffled by the question. Then he realized she meant was he going to punish her. "Nothing," he said.

"You're not going to send me away?"

"Why would I do that? I risked my neck to get you back."

"Maybe now you wish you hadn't," she suggested, her voice wobbling.

Pod felt a twist of sorrow and guilt. "You're my sister," he said. "Getting you back is all I've thought about since the day they took you."

Abruptly, she put her arms around his neck and hugged him fiercely. Slightly surprised, but relieved, Pod hugged her back. "Tell them I'm sorry," she said in a harsh whisper.

Pod went back up on deck and handed out the missing objects.

"She won't do it again," he said. "She's sorry."

"Why did she do it?" asked Essie.

Pod thought for a moment about how to explain it. "Cruise ships," he said finally. "Lots of poor people locked up with lots of rich people."

"We're not rich," Will said. "Except for Essie. She's rich."

"Don't tell *her* that," Essie said with a grin.

Pod looked embarrassed all over again.

Annalie felt sorry for him. "She just needs to get to know us a bit better," she said. "Let's forget it ever happened."

Graham makes a contribution

Nothing more did go missing, and the weeks that followed were marked by a series of storms which made for some less-than-pleasant sailing. But the strong winds that brought the storms also helped them on their way, and one day they came unexpectedly on their first sign that Sundia was close by.

Will was the first one to spot the floating object. "What do you think that is?" he asked.

"Some sort of buoy," Annalie said.

"Pretty big buoy," Will said.

"Is it for fishing?" Essie suggested. "Some kind of marker?"

"It's got a solar panel on it," Pod pointed out. "Why would it need a solar panel?"

"Is it a scientific instrument?" Annalie suggested. "Maybe it measures the waves or something."

"I know what it's for," Will said suddenly. "It's part of Sundia's coastal defenses. I read something about this in that stuff you found, Essie. There'll be more of these, up and down the coast. I think they're all emitting a signal, and if you cross the signal and interrupt it, it sends a warning to the coastguard."

"Then how are we going to get to shore without letting them know we're here?" Annalie asked.

"Do we risk it and hope that by the time they can send a ship after us we're already gone?" Essie suggested.

"Pretty big risk," Annalie said.

"Maybe we could disable the beacon," Pod suggested.

A thoughtful look appeared on Will's face. "Maybe," he said.

Will paddled out with his mask and flippers to look at the buoy. He didn't dare take the *Sunfish* any closer, or even the dinghy, for fear of tripping the alert, but he guessed a swimmer in the water would probably go undetected.

He swam around the buoy, wondering if it would be possible to simply detach it from its mooring. A solid metal chain held it in place, and he had nothing on the boat that would cut through that sort of metal. He began to examine the buoy itself. There was an access panel in the side, but it had been tightly sealed. To get it open, he'd have to rip out the side of the buoy, and he was still hoping he could disable it without creating any obvious signs of sabotage.

He turned his attention to the solar panel on top. Perhaps there was some way to damage or disable it to stop the buoy from recharging. He knew it must have a battery so it could keep running at night when the sun wasn't shining, but the battery life couldn't last all that long, right? He looked for relays he could decouple, a panel he could prise loose or smash, but the couplings were all tucked away inside the buoy, and the panel was protected by a tough weatherproof housing. He could have taken a hammer to it. But again, not subtle.

He studied the buoy for a moment longer, thinking. Then his eye was caught by a long white streak of bird poo that dribbled down the side. And he had a brilliant idea.

"You want Graham to poo on the solar panel?" Pod repeated.

Essie had dissolved into hopeless giggles.

"It'll take a lot of poo to cover the whole panel," Annalie said.

"Graham not poo on demand," Graham said haughtily.

Will turned to Annalie. "Which foods make him really squirty?" he asked.

"You'd need something that came out with a thick consistency," Annalie said thoughtfully. "Otherwise you're not going to get the coverage."

"I can't believe you're discussing the consistency of Graham's poo," Essie said.

"Graham not say yes," Graham reminded them.

"Come on, Graham, you don't usually care where

140

you let them go," Will said. "Why not poo somewhere that will actually help us for a change?"

Grudgingly, Graham agreed to stuff himself with food, then fly over to the buoy and wait for the results. They ended up having to do this several times before they had a thick enough coating on the solar panel. Then all they had to do was wait until the tiny winking green light on the side of the buoy stopped working. Late that night, the light went off—the buoy was dark. They sailed into Sundia's territorial waters.

The Skeleton Coast

Will was at the wheel as they sailed toward the still-distant shore. Annalie came to join him. The air began to grow perceptibly damper and colder.

"Feel that?" Will said.

All around them, the starlight grew hazy. Then it disappeared.

"Fog," Will said.

"We're going to have to be extra careful from now on," Annalie said. "They call this the Skeleton Coast."

"That's here?"

"Uh-huh. Rocks, reefs, and fog. It's a bad combination."

"What are our charts like?"

"Out of date," Annalie said. "Pre-Flood."

"That's got to be good news, right? Some of the rocks and reefs are further underwater now. Not so much stuff to hit."

"Maybe," Annalie said. "Maybe not."

The Skeleton Coast was one of the more notorious regions of the Sundian coastline. Its treacherous conditions had made it a graveyard of ships for the early sailors from the north; many ran aground on reefs they couldn't see in the fog, and those sailors who made it into longboats and got ashore found themselves pinned on the stony beaches between the pounding surf of the Outer Ocean and the vast immensity of the desert, unable to escape.

The next day, the fog was still there; as they sailed, they discovered that it rarely lifted, blanketing the coastline, making it impossible to see the shore. Where possible, Will skirted the edge of the fog rather than sailing through it—it was too exhausting and too dangerous to sail through it for hours at a time, eyes struggling to penetrate the shifting amorphous grayness. The rocks and reefs were a very real danger—easy enough to see in the daytime but harder to see at night—and the charts were not a reliable guide. It felt sometimes that they were feeling their way south, sailing by hand and eye.

They drew up a roster; even Blossom was forced to do her share of keeping watch, and it was she who discovered one of the other ways the Sundians protected their coastline.

"What's that thing in the water?" she called to Will, who was at the wheel. She had spotted another floating object, different from the signal buoy.

"Where?" Will asked, coming to look.

Blossom pointed. Will looked, then ran back to the wheel and spun it hard. The boom swung; the boat began to turn. Something tipped over down in the saloon, and Annalie came up to see what was the matter.

"Everything okay?" she said.

"There are mines," Will said. "Look!"

Annalie ran to the railing where Blossom was standing. She watched in horror as the *Sunfish* sailed past a huge, round, spiky object floating on the surface of the water.

"Are you sure that's a mine?" she asked.

Essie had come to join her. "That's what they look like in old war movies."

"I bet that's not the only one," Will said.

"What would have happened if we'd hit it?" Blossom asked.

"Ka-boom!" Will said, his hands flying up expressively.

After that, they steered clear of the fog; the risk of crossing the electronic barrier seemed less immediate than the risk of crashing into a mine. But this carried other dangers too: once they were out of the fog, they could be seen.

One day, Graham raised the alarm.

"What is it?" Pod asked, grabbing the binoculars.

"A ship!" Graham said, as the others came running.

"Sundian coastguard?" Will said.

"I think—" Pod said, and stopped. He handed the binoculars to Annalie, who was standing next to him.

"Oh no."

"Who is it?" Will asked.

"It's the Admiralty."

The Cauldron

The Admiralty ship was still far away on the horizon, but there was no mistaking it. It was the same boat they'd encountered in Dio, the boat that had carried Beckett halfway around the world in pursuit of them. And now here it was again.

"Do you think it's the same ship?" asked Essie.

"It has to be," Will said.

"How did they find us?" Annalie wailed.

"They're the Admiralty," Pod said. "That's what they do."

"What are we going to do?" asked Essie.

"I don't think we've got a choice," Will said grimly. "We try and lose them in the fog."

They sailed into the veil of fog. The grayness closed around them, cold, bleak, disorienting. "Everybody watch out for rocks!" Will ordered.

Pod, Essie, even Blossom took positions around the deck and watched the water. Will sailed on as fast as he dared.

"Be really careful," Annalie warned, checking the charts. "There's a thing called the Cauldron somewhere near our position."

"What is it?"

"I'm not exactly sure, but they warn us to stay away from it."

Not long afterwards, Will noticed a telltale droning sound. "Can you hear that?"

Annalie listened. "Sounds like an engine."

"They're coming after us."

The sound began to build, but the fog was so thick that they could see nothing. Suddenly, an inflatable boat filled with heavily armed marines appeared out of the fog. Will expected them to hail him, as they had done every other time he'd encountered them, but these marines said nothing at all. They just took up a position to their rear and kept pace with them.

"What are they doing?" Essie called fearfully.

"I don't know," Will said.

For a minute or two, they sailed along and the inflatable kept pace. Then the inflatable dropped back astern; they heard a distant crack, and something came whistling across their bows.

Will let out a startled cry and turned the wheel sharply.

"What was that?" Annalie gasped.

"They're shooting at us!" Essie cried.

"It's a rope!" Pod called from the bow.

The inflatable zipped back into view and took a pass around the *Sunfish* to see what had happened. This time, Will could see a marine with a radio reporting back.

"Why would they shoot a rope at us?" he muttered.

The sound of engines multiplied; a second inflatable

emerged from the fog and joined them.

"Why aren't they boarding us?" Annalie said, perturbed.

The dinghies spun away from the *Sunfish* and they heard the same distant crack. Something flew across the deck, nearly taking Will's head off. He crashed to the ground and saw that a huge grappling hook on a steel cable had crossed their bows and hooked itself onto the railing around the edge of the deck.

"We're hooked!" Will said grimly. "I bet they're going to try and pull us in."

"We've got to get unhooked!" Annalie cried.

"We'll never cut that cable," Essie said.

"Then cut the railing!" Will shouted. "Annalie! Take the wheel!"

Annalie took the wheel while Will ran to grab an ax. Desperately he swung it into the railing with a dull thunk of metal on metal. The *Sunfish* creaked and groaned as the sails pulled it one way, the cable another. *Clang! Clang!* Will's arms were getting numb. *Creak!* The *Sunfish* moaned.

"Look!" Pod shrieked. "Up ahead!"

From out of the swirling gray, a huge shape had suddenly materialized: a vast rocky headland, looming directly in their path.

"That's our chance!" Will shouted.

He dropped the ax with a clatter, ran back to the wheel, grabbed onto it with Annalie, and swung it as hard as it would go. The *Sunfish* turned. It skimmed the edge of the rocks, and the rope that tethered it to the Admiralty warship struck the headland. For a moment it hung there, straining across the rocky outcrop, then with a terrible tearing sound, the whole railing ripped away. Annalie and Will dropped to the deck again in the nick of time as it broke free and went swinging off into the ocean, barely skimming their heads and only just missing the wheel.

Pod, Essie, and Blossom came hurrying back to join Will and Annalie, keeping clear of the large gap in the railing.

"Let's hope this rock gives us some cover," Will said.

"Those little boats are still coming after us," Essie reported.

"Let's see how fast we can go then," Will said. "Guys, get the sails down, quick."

He switched to engine power as Essie and Pod rushed to bring in the sails.

Annalie was studying the charts. "I could be wrong," she said, "but I think we're sailing into the Cauldron. There are some islands off the mainland, and a channel that runs between them. The Cauldron lies somewhere in that channel."

"Sounds like that place Spinner told us about— the one in the legend, where if you sail between the rocks at the wrong time, you get sucked down and smashed by a whirlpool."

"Right," Annalie said, remembering the story. "Only that isn't a legend, it's a real place."

"Oh, great! Now you tell me!" Will said.

"Look at that current," Annalie said.

The current was ferocious, and they were hurtling

through the water, rocks on one side of them, the invisible shore on the other. Somewhere out to sea, the Admiralty ship lay in wait. The two inflatables filled with marines were still cruising on their tail.

"As soon as we get around this island, they're going to have another go at us," Annalie warned, still studying the chart.

"We've got bigger problems," Will said. "Look."

The current was running faster and faster toward an area of turbulent water. As they got closer, they could see it was beginning to spin, as if someone had pulled a plug out of the ocean.

"Look at that thing," Annalie said. "It's like a centrifuge."

"They only do that at high tide," Will said.

"Trust us to come along at just the wrong time."

"Or the right time," Will said.

"We've got to turn back!" Annalie said.

"Not a chance," Will said.

"If we get caught in it, it could break us apart or sink us!"

"We won't sink," Will said. "The *Sunfish* can handle it."

"No!" Annalie cried, but Will had already made up his mind. He kept moving forward, directly into the growing whirlpool. Annalie looked back and saw the two inflatables circle back and hover, staying clear of the powerful current, their engines working hard to keep in place. It made her even more frightened of what they were getting into when she realized even hardened marines were not willing to risk it.

"Guys! Get hold of something and hang on!" Will yelled.

The others ran to find a safe handhold, and then they were into the whirlpool. The water swirled and rushed around them. The boat creaked and groaned and strained. Will struggled to keep control of the steering, but the force of the water was dragging them broadside, the current beating at them.

"Look!" Essie cried.

Annalie looked back and, to her disbelief, saw that one of the inflatables had decided to come after them. "They're relentless!" she whispered.

The *Sunfish* struggled, timbers groaning as the extreme force of the whirlpool battered her sides; she tilted, pushed sideways by the current, and water started rushing over the deck.

"Hang on! This is going to get even bumpier!" Will yelled.

He motored on through the turbulence, water rushing and smashing at them. Behind them, the inflatable cut through the whirlpool as it turned faster and faster. Then all of a sudden, the inflatable was caught by a curl of the current; it tipped, then flew up into the air and landed upside down.

"They're in the water!" Annalie cried.

"There's nothing we can do for them," Will said. "We'll be lucky if we get across this thing ourselves."

He fought on, across the swirling water.

"I think we're going to make it," he said.

"Don't jinx us!" Pod said.

But Will was right. The force of the water was

150

already lessening. The current was slowing. They had made it through the Cauldron.

Annalie was still looking back, worried about what had happened to the other marines. "The second inflatable's going in to help," she reported. "There are a lot of marines in the water. They're going to have to call for back up. It could take them ages to find them all."

"That's what I'm hoping for," Will said. "While they're doing a rescue mission, we can get away. Come and keep an eye on these charts. I'm going to take us right in close to shore."

In moments, the island, the whirlpool, and the inflatables had vanished once more into the fog. Will switched the noisy motor off and they raced to raise the sails once more, then he steered as close to shore as he dared. Pod, Essie, and Blossom kept a lookout for rocks, Annalie following the charts. They sailed like this for many hours, their ears straining for the sound of engines, but they heard nothing but the boom of the surf and the occasional cry of a seabird. The strange thing about sailing through fog was that they had no idea how far or how fast they were going. The boat was in motion, pushed by the wind and the waves, but sometimes it felt like they were trapped in a bottle, being shaken by a giant, and were not really going anywhere at all.

"It's no use," Annalie said finally. "I have no idea where we are."

"What do you reckon?" Will said. "Do we stick our heads out and look?"

"We're going to have to at some point," Annalie said. "Or we might hit something."

Essie looked over at them. "What if Beckett's still out there?"

"Let's find out," Will said.

They sailed cautiously out of the fog. The late afternoon sun as it struck them was like a blessing.

The ocean stretched out all around them, sunlit, empty.

"I think we lost them," Will said, and smiled.

Kinlemotukinle

Expecting Beckett's ship to appear again at any moment, they sailed as fast as they could down the coast of Sundia. The clinging fog faded as they traveled south, revealing stark red desert, and the wind that blew off it was baking hot. But as they traveled still farther south, they began to see signs of life emerge from the intense red of the desert. Coast scrub—green and silver and white—promised water, birds, and people too.

The west coast of Sundia was famous for its high cliffs and pounding surf, which made it difficult to get ashore except in a few rare places. The town that serviced the Ark was one place—it was set on a little inlet—but they had decided going into the town was too risky. Instead, they would go ashore at a place called Kinle Bay.

Kinle Bay was a natural harbor almost exactly due west of the Ark. It had once been a tourist destination of sorts—it was the site of an old temple to Kinlemotukinle, a sea god in the form of a hunting fish. The temple was one of the last remnants of an early Sundian city which had collapsed for reasons which were now unclear—possibly a drought. The site, even pre-Flood, was rarely visited—it was too remote for most tourists to bother with, and even the Sundians didn't go there much. Annalie and Will hoped that it was still mostly deserted and the wide shallow bay would be somewhere safe to leave the *Sunfish* while they went ashore. Its relative proximity to the Ark also meant that the distance they'd have to travel overland was pleasingly short.

And how beautiful it was! The bay was wide and blue and lovely, and the shoreline was a mixture of tall, rocky outcrops and verdant greenery growing almost to the water's edge.

"Does it look like people might live here?" Will asked.

They were all on deck, scanning the foreshore. There were no boats, no houses, no signs that anyone lived here apart from birds.

"Graham, can you go and check it out for us?" Will asked.

Graham went winging around the bay, disappearing over the treetops. A pair of small angry birds popped up out of the treetops and chased him, screeching.

"Locals only, huh?" Will said. "Everywhere's the same."

While everyone else was watching the birds or the shoreline, Essie's eye was caught by something moving in the water. She only glimpsed it for a second, but whatever it was, it seemed big. "Did you see that?" she asked.

"See what?" said Will.

"I thought I saw something in the water ... Probably nothing."

A few minutes passed, and Graham returned. "Big temple," he reported. "Nothing else. Just rocks and trees."

They sailed in a little closer to shore, and as they came around a small headland, the temple of Kinlemotukinle was revealed.

"Whoa," Essie said.

"I didn't realize it was going to be *that* big," Annalie said.

The temple was built out of enormous slabs of rock. Some of it was the same local rock that lined the cliffs and rolled down to the sea, but some of it was entirely different rock, obtained from who knows where. Washed up by storms? Transported from elsewhere? These enormous rocks had been stacked upon each other into great imposing columns to make the shape of the temple, while others had been beautifully carved into ornaments and statues.

"*Look!*" Blossom cried.

The motion of the boat had gradually moved them into the perfect position to look straight down the avenue of columns and reveal the largest statue of all. It had been carved ingeniously out of more than one piece of stone to create a figure that was easily twenty feet high. At the bottom of the figure, a huge fish with sharp, pointed teeth reared up out of flowing stone waves, savage and lively, as if it had leaped out of the water for sheer joy. A second figure emerged from this fish, perhaps stepping from its mouth, perhaps captured in the moment of changing its form from fish to human. This figure was grandly, lithely muscular in the way that only a god could be, stepping from the waves in a swirl of long hair and fine robes, one arm outstretched to point toward the sea, its square face fierce and beautiful.

"It's the Lucky Lady!" Blossom breathed.

"I think that's meant to be the sea god as a hunting fish," Essie said.

"Is that a fish?" Will said. "Or do you think it's a shark?"

"It's the Lucky Lady, I know it is," Blossom said stubbornly.

"Well, anyway, this looks like the place," Annalie said. "Let's go ashore."

They anchored in the bay, and Will began dragging out the pieces of the thing he had been working on for weeks. There was a set of wheels, something that looked like a pair of huge skis, a frame with a light platform, and a sail.

"*Now* are you going to tell us what that is?" Annalie said.

"Can't you guess?" Will said, grinning. "It's a land surfer."

"A what?" said Annalie.

"I got the idea from one of those old tourist books," Will said. "They used to go land-surfing on the dunes. The picture wasn't that great and I couldn't tell whether they surfed on wheels or on runners. So I made both."

"That sounds way better than walking," Annalie said. "I hope it works."

"Of course it'll work," Will said scornfully.

They loaded the dinghy with everything they'd need for the trip to the Ark—packs and tools and hats and water and provisions—and the five of them climbed carefully aboard. The dinghy was heavily loaded once everyone was aboard and it rode dangerously low in the water.

"Are you sure we shouldn't do this in two trips?" Annalie asked.

"It's not far, and there's not much surf," Will said. "We'll be fine."

He started the engine and steered the dinghy toward the shore, Graham flying overhead.

They hadn't gone far when they heard Graham shriek.

"What's up with him?" Pod asked.

"Probably those stupid local birds again," Will said.

But it wasn't the birds.

Moments later, something slammed into the dinghy. It rocked but miraculously stayed afloat.

"What happened?" Annalie cried.

"Did we hit something?" Essie said.

"Something hit us," Will said.

Graham was still shrieking overhead. Blossom saw it first. She screamed, speechless, pointing.

A large fin was coming toward them, accelerating fast. As it came closer, a black-and-white back appeared above the water.

"Everybody hang on!" Will shouted. He accelerated, turning at the last moment in a bid to evade their attacker. They skimmed past without making contact, but the fin disappeared below the water and they knew it was turning for another pass.

"What was that?" Pod cried.

"A shadow whale," Will said. "The biggest and most aggressive of the hunting whales."

"But why's it attacking us?" Essie said. "Do they normally do that?"

"Not usually," Will said. "Hang on. Here it comes again!"

The shadow whale was accelerating toward them once more, and this time it was ready for Will's maneuvers. It followed his twists and turns with fluid ease, then flipped the dinghy up into the air. For a terrible moment they were all aloft, the people, the packs, the equipment, and then they were splashing down into the water. Pod and Blossom were the only ones wearing life jackets; the others had decided not to bother when they were only a hundred yards or so from the shore.

Will had managed to stay clinging to the dinghy when it flipped; miraculously, it had landed the right way up, but the motor had stalled. "Swim to me!" he yelled. "Quick!"

Essie was the first to swim up to the dinghy and was over the side like lightning.

"Help the others," Will said quickly. "I'm going after the gear."

"What?" Essie cried. "Stay in the boat! That thing's trying to eat us!"

"We can't get across the desert without gear," Will said. "It's not very deep. I'm going down for it."

To Essie's horror, Will went over the side. She looked for the others and saw Blossom flailing in the water, hyperventilating in terror. Pod was paddling awkwardly toward her, held up by his life jacket. Annalie was the furthest from the boat but swimming back.

"It's okay, Blossom," gasped Pod. "I'll help you."

He reached Blossom and the two of them began floundering in the general direction of the dinghy, but they were not really getting anywhere.

Essie looked around for a rope. Where was the rope? It had probably been flung overboard along with everything else.

Will surfaced and tossed a pack into the dinghy. He took a deep breath and disappeared underwater again.

"Use your arms," Essie shouted to Pod and Blossom. "Quick!"

Graham, still circling above them, shrieked out a warning. The whale came at them again in a great rush, surfing between Pod and Blossom and the dinghy and then swatting them into deeper water with a lazy swipe of its tail.

Annalie reached the dinghy and pulled herself aboard. "Where's Will? What's wrong with the engine?"

"Will's diving for the gear," Essie said. "I don't know what's wrong with the engine."

Annalie frowned and looked at it, trying to get it working.

"Come on!" Essie pleaded, looking at the others. "Hurry!"

159

Will surfaced again with more gear. He slopped it into the dinghy.

"Forget the gear! Get back in the boat!" Essie shouted, but he had already dived under again.

With a splutter, the engine started. "I'm coming around to pick you up," Annalie shouted to Pod and Blossom. She motored slowly over to them while Essie kept a lookout for the whale, and then the two of them dragged Pod and Blossom aboard. "Let's get Will and get out of here," Essie said.

Will had popped up again on the surface and was treading water with some of the pieces of his land surfer. Annalie steered over to him and he tossed the gear into the dinghy.

"Leave it behind," she said. "We can't stay out here with that thing in the water."

"We need our gear or we won't make it across the desert," Will insisted. "Take the others to shore, then come back for me."

"Will, this is a bad idea!" Annalie shouted.

"Go!" Will roared, and dived once more.

Seeing it was pointless to argue with him, Annalie gunned the dinghy and raced for the shore. The whale came after them, straight as an arrow, but this time, they were too fast for it. Annalie slowed to a stop in the shallow water. "Take the gear! Run! I'm going back for Will!" she cried.

They hurled the gear out of the boat and scrambled up onto the safety of the rocks while Annalie turned again and zoomed out to where Will's head bobbed in the water. But the whale had other ideas. It reared up out of the water, scooping Will up hard with its head. Will went flying and hit the water with a smack, the sail he was holding spinning away. Annalie chased after him, scooping the sail up as she went, as Will disappeared below the surface. Why wasn't he coming up? Had the whale grabbed him and pulled him under? She tightened her grip on the sail and heard Graham once again, calling from above her. In the clear waters of the bay, he had the perfect vantage point. Annalie followed his lead until she saw the black-and-white shape below her; she braced herself against the dinghy and jabbed down with the end of the sail's mast. It was no harpoon, but she landed a solid blow; she knew she must have hurt it. In a flurry of water and bubbles, Will suddenly floated to the surface. She grabbed him and frantically dragged him into the dinghy.

She turned for what she hoped was the last time and headed for the shore. She could hear the others yelling; she guessed the whale was chasing her. She could not think about that. She drove the dinghy up as far as she dared, right up onto the rocks, hoping she wasn't tearing the bottom out of it. She pulled Will up from the bottom of the dinghy and clambered over the front, dragging her brother with her. Behind them, she glimpsed the enormous whale surfing up onto the rocks, its huge mouth open, rows of teeth glinting. A bow-wave of water broke over her as the whale snapped at her in a fury, almost biting the engine off the dinghy, before it wriggled back into the water.

"Will! Are you okay?!" she cried desperately, as Pod came hurrying to help her.

He was wet and pale, his eyes closed, and she feared that the whale had drowned him. But then he heaved up seawater and coughed and spluttered, and his eyes opened and he looked around.

"Did we make it?" he coughed.

"We made it," Annalie said, so relieved she had tears in her eyes.

They helped Will to his feet and tottered up the rocks to where Essie and Blossom were waiting with Graham and the gear.

"What was all that about?" Essie asked. "Don't they normally just eat fish?"

"They eat seals too," Will said. "Maybe it thought we were seals."

"No," Blossom said. "It was guarding the temple."

The others all turned to stare at her.

"Look," Blossom said. She turned to point at the colossal central figure of the temple. It was obvious now that the figure was half human, half shadow whale. "I *told* you not to annoy the sea gods."

The ruined city

"You do know that whale wasn't *really* defending the temple," Will argued as they carried their remaining gear up to the temple floor. "It's ridiculous. Why would it do that?"

"I think there *are* some stories of shadow whales cooperating with humans," Annalie said thoughtfully. "Although I think it was mostly to get fish."

"There. You see?" Will said. "This temple hasn't been used for centuries, so why would the whale still be defending it?"

"Think what you like," Blossom said stubbornly. "I know what I know."

"Okay, let's see how much of our gear made it to shore," Pod said, eager to change the subject.

Two of the packs were gone, and with them water bottles and food. Will had rescued most of his land surfer, although the skis hadn't made it.

"If the wheels won't go through soft sand, we're stuffed," he said gloomily.

"You're not going back for the missing bits," Annalie warned.

"Don't worry, I'm not going back in that water in a hurry," Will said.

"We can walk if we have to," Essie said. "Although personally, I'd rather not."

"It's a long walk in the sun," Pod said. "If the land surfer won't work, we should wait until night time."

"I agree," Annalie said. "It's at least two days on foot. If we do it at night, it'll be cooler and we won't use up so much water. Once we're out there, I don't think there'll be any way to get more."

"The land surfer will work," Will insisted crossly. "Let's get out of this place and work out where we're going."

He hoisted himself to his feet and began parceling out the stuff for everyone to carry.

"Wait, aren't we going to make an offering to the Lady first?" Blossom asked.

"What?" Will said.

"We need to ask for her protection," Blossom said.

Will lost his temper. "Let's get one thing straight. The only thing protecting us here is us. Not lucky ladies, not sea gods. Us. Okay? We don't have time to make offerings. We're leaving."

A look of pure rage spread over Blossom's face. "How can you say that after what just happened?" she shouted.

"Let's go," Will snapped, and walked away.

Annalie and Essie hesitated, looking at Pod and Blossom. "Coming?" asked Annalie.

"In a minute," Pod said.

As the girls walked away, Blossom raged at Pod.

"Does he want to end up dead? Because that's what's going to happen, and he'll drag us into it, too."

"You have to understand, not everybody believes in the Lucky Lady," Pod said.

"How can you not believe in her?" Blossom cried. "Look at this place!"

"All Will sees is an old temple," Pod said. "He doesn't believe in gods."

"What about you? You know better, right?"

Pod hesitated. Blossom's face fell. "Oh."

"Come on," Pod said coaxingly. "We don't want to get left behind."

"No!" Blossom shouted. "You go with your friends if you want to. *I'm* going to make an offering."

And she stormed off in the opposite direction.

Pod hesitated for a moment, knowing he should go after her. *Why does she have to be so stubborn?* he thought crossly, remembering all the other times she'd refused to be part of the team.

Fine. If she wants to do her own thing, let her, he thought.

And he turned to follow Will and the others.

He walked out of the temple and into the ruins of an ancient city, now little more than tumbled stone, with trees growing up thickly among the old walls, weeds growing where roads had once been. It seemed to him that he was only a minute or two behind the others. But there was no sign of them.

A path seemed to lead into the ruins. *This must be the way they went*, he thought, and followed it, hoping to catch up with them around the next bend.

But there was no sign of them around the next bend, or the next.

Where were they?

"Where are they?"

Belatedly, Will, Annalie, and Essie had realized that Pod and Blossom were not behind them. The ruins stretched out like a maze, larger than the tourist material and their maps had suggested.

"Graham find them?" Graham suggested.

"Wait, we can't be far from the edge of town," Will said. "You can feel the desert."

He was right; although the ruined city was cool and green, they could feel the desert's hot breath.

"Let's get out of these ruins. Then I can build my surfer while we wait for them to catch up," Will said.

They walked on. The trees thinned; the soil became sand. The red desert stretched out ahead, shimmering in the heat.

"Feel that?" Annalie said, dismayed. "We're going to miss those extra water bottles."

"Graham find Pod now?" Graham said.

"You might as well," Will said. Graham took off. "Don't get lost!" Will called after him. A derisory screech drifted back to them.

"There must be water here somewhere," Annalie said thoughtfully. "You couldn't build a city like this and live here without water."

"City was abandoned though, wasn't it?" Will said. "Maybe that's why."

"But look how green it is," Annalie said. "It can't just be rainfall keeping these trees alive. I wonder if there's ground water? Or a spring?" She paused. "I'm going to see if I can find it while we wait for the others."

"I'll come with you," said Essie.

Will was already looking for a shady spot to start building his land surfer. "Sure, whatever," he said.

Graham flew over the ruins, looking for Pod. Earlier, there had been birds around. Now there was no sign of them. He sensed they were there still, hiding in the trees, listening, silent. Listening for what? Hiding from what?

Graham had a bad feeling about this place. He glided on.

My jewel. That's what I should have given her.

Blossom was looking for something to leave as an offering. It would need to be something special to keep them safe, after what Will had said. Her jewel was her favorite—it would have been perfect—but it was back on the boat. She felt through her pockets, just in case. She always carried useful things, and sometimes one or two treasures, just to keep them close, but this time she found nothing worthy.

She arrived at a place where the walls stood higher than most. Trees grew up inside them, but she could see that once this had been something fine and important. She lifted aside trailing vines and crept in under the branches, looking around her. Another temple? She went deeper in, and caught sight of something marvelous. A partial wall, covered in human figures—women dancing—made out of colored stones and pieces of shell pressed into the wall. She ran up to them and ran her fingers over them; how beautiful they were! They would make the perfect gift for the Lady; but how to offer them without tearing them from the wall? She knew that damaging this lovely thing, even to give it to the Lady, would not win her favor. She took a step back and felt the ground crunching slightly under her feet. She looked down; pieces of the fresco had broken off and fallen to the floor. Most were crumbled, unrecognisable, but she found one good-sized piece with a recognisable human eye pressed into it. She picked it up. It gazed back at her.

Yes. This was the thing.

She turned back to the temple.

"Will?" Pod called. "Annalie?"

He was still walking, hot, tired, sick of the ruins. There was no sign of the others, and no sign of Blossom.

The trees that grew everywhere had fine needles instead of leaves, and when the wind blew through them, as it did frequently, it made a shushing, moaning, sibilant sound he was starting to find a bit creepy.

A great screech echoed off the rocks and Graham came fluttering down to land on a branch above him. "Found you!" Graham said. "Where Little Pod?"

"She wandered off."

Graham made a disapproving noise.

"I know," Pod sighed. "We'd better find the others. Then maybe you can help me track her down."

Graham rarked an affirmative and spread his wings to take off again, but then something caught his eye. He froze in place, looking into the undergrowth.

"What is it?" Pod asked uneasily.

"Something there," Graham said in his harsh voice.

Pod was already spooked enough by the whale attack and Blossom's talk of bad luck. He turned to look at the undergrowth, but saw nothing. "What sort of something?"

"Don't know. Let's go."

Graham took off. Pod hurried after him. The bird flew ahead, now soaring up for a better vantage point, now circling around behind.

"It following us," he reported.

"What's following us?"

"Can't tell. Too sneaky."

Pod stopped. "What kind of thing, Graham?" he demanded.

Graham screeched at him. He had no better answer to give.

Pod suddenly had the horrible feeling that letting Blossom go off on her own had been a big mistake. "We have to find Blossom!"

"I knew it!" Annalie crowed. Sure enough, in the deepest, greenest part of the ruins, a little spring emerged from the ground and made a pool; a stream trickled away from it and lost itself among rocks and thick underbrush. Annalie scooped the water into her mouth. "It's good," she said.

"Shouldn't you be boiling it first, or filtering it?" Essie asked.

"*You* can," Annalie said, scooping up more water thirstily.

Essie shrugged and joined her. They both drank until their stomachs were full.

"Lots of aquifers got salty when the ocean rose," Annalie said, wiping her mouth. "Lucky this one's still okay."

"Did you hear that?" Essie said suddenly.

"What?"

"It all just went super-quiet."

It *had* all just gone super-quiet. The birds had stopped. The insects had stopped. The wind moaned briefly, and then that stopped too.

In the silence, a twig snapped.

Then the undergrowth stirred and something stepped out. It was a dog, medium-sized, lean and red-brown, the color of the desert. It stared at them, hard-eyed.

Instinctively, Annalie and Essie drew closer together. "I don't think that dog looks very friendly," Essie whispered.

The dog lifted its snout and let out a spiraling, howling call.

Another howl came in answer. Then another.

"If you can find a sharp stick, grab one," Annalie muttered.

Cautiously, they reached for whatever was around them. Annalie found a rock; Essie's hand closed around a stick. They got slowly to their feet.

The dog curled its lip and snarled at them.

They began to back away from the waterhole, one step at a time.

The dog howled again; something prompted Essie to turn around. A second huge dog leaped at her. Letting out a cry, she fended it off with the stick just in time, and it twisted away from her with a squeal.

"Run!" Essie cried.

Blossom walked down the wide colonnade of the temple.

The cool stone columns rose up on either side of her, and her feet echoed faintly on the stone paving. It was very quiet; all she could hear was the gentle shush of the wind moving through the trees.

She walked right up to the foot of the statue and gazed up at the fierce, kind, savage, beautiful face of the lady.

Lucky Lady, she thought, forming the words very clearly and distinctly in her mind. *Please help me. Me and my brother. Keep us safe from danger and find us somewhere good to live.* She paused, then thought, *Preferably not by the sea.*

She placed her offering carefully on a wave-shaped niche. *Oh, and could you please help the others, too,* she added, a little grudgingly.

She stood there a moment longer, and the air about her seemed to thicken and become charged, almost magical. She felt something stirring inside her. Was it really happening? Was this the touch of the Lucky Lady?

A shout rang out: "Blossom, behind you!"

It was Pod's voice. She spun around and saw a lean reddish-black dog, all fangs and hungry eyes, stalking toward her up the colonnade. She froze.

Graham, screeching angrily, swooped down on the dog, claws outstretched, raking at its face. The dog was momentarily distracted, and Pod yelled: "Blossom! This way! Run!"

Pod was holding out his hand to her, scared but brave. Jolted from her trance, she ran to him. They leaped from the temple and began to run through the trees, the dog coming after them.

"Where are the others?" she asked, panting.

"Hopefully waiting for us somewhere safe," Pod said.

Essie and Annalie scrambled up a tree. It was not a very tall tree and it was swaying beneath their weight.

"What is up with this place?" Essie gasped. "Killer whales, wild dogs ..."

The two wild dogs arrived at the base of the tree and began to pace back and forth, looking up at them, hungry, cunning, patient. As they perched there, a third appeared out of the trees.

"Do you think they'll get sick of it and go away?" Essie asked.

"Nope," Annalie said.

Graham came circling out of the sky and looped around their heads.

"Graham, thank goodness!" Annalie said. "You've got to warn Will—"

"Graham knows. Graham going."

"Tell him to bring rocks!" Essie called after him.

Down below, one of the dogs had stiffened and turned away from the clearing, looking back into the trees, his ears flat. He barked once and the other dogs came to join him.

"They've seen something," Annalie said.

"It could be Pod."

"Or Blossom," Annalie said, and shouted a warning. "Look out! There are wild dogs! Run!"

A yell split the air, but it was not the sound of someone running away. Pod and Blossom burst from the undergrowth, yelling like banshees. To Annalie's utter amazement, they were brandishing huge branches tipped with flaming needles. They ran at the dogs, swinging their branches ferociously. The flames crackled and spat, the smoke swirled; the dogs snarled at them, but together Pod and Blossom drove them back toward the trees.

Seizing their chance, Essie and Annalie tumbled down from the tree. "This way! Come on!" Essie called.

Pod took one last swipe at the dogs and began to run. Blossom, who had found an appetite for the work, had to be dragged away. Then all four of them were off, running headlong for the edge of the trees.

"Are they following us?" Annalie said.

Pod glanced back; the dogs were still coming after them, but as he looked, they all seemed to obey some signal and vanished from the path into the trees.

"Uh-oh," he said. "I think they're going to try and cut us off."

They kept running helter-skelter down the path, Essie in front, Pod and Blossom a little behind. They ran through the last trees and tumbled stones, and just as they were about to emerge into the open, the largest and fiercest of the dogs, the huge reddish-black animal that had stalked Blossom in the temple, came racing up the side of a rock and launched itself directly at her.

Time seemed to slow down.

Pod saw the dog hurtling toward his sister's throat, teeth bared.

He heard Annalie cry out.

He began to swing the stick that he held, knowing it would not connect in time.

Then there was an enormous *donk* and the dog seemed to change direction in midair.

A rock had flown out of nowhere and hit it.

"Quick!" Annalie shouted.

And then they were running again, Pod and Blossom, and they were out of the trees, and the remaining dogs were coming after them, but Annalie and Will were already aboard a strange thing that looked part canoe, part sailing vessel, part wheelbarrow, and Essie was standing in the path, a great big rock in her hand. It was Essie who had thrown the first rock and was waiting with another in case the dogs wanted to have another try. The rest of the dogs had thought better of it and were circling beside their fallen companion, still hostile but wary, and Will was shouting, "Quick, get aboard!" and Essie, Pod and Blossom all ran to jump on.

Will kicked off, angling the sail to catch the wind. The wheels began to turn, and the land surfer began to lumber forward. Not fast enough, not at all fast enough, and one dog then another began pacing toward them, sensing a meal, but then Will caught a lucky wind gust, the surfer jerked forward more quickly, and they were off, sailing out into the red desert.

The dogs could still have caught up with them, but perhaps they didn't have the heart for a long chase through the desert. As they sailed into the sun, the dogs gave up; soon, they had vanished back into the trees once more.

"I was kind of afraid this thing wasn't going to work," Annalie said when they could all breathe once more.

"What do you mean?" Will said indignantly. "It was always going to work!"

"I can't believe what you guys did," Essie said, turning to Pod and Blossom. "Taking on those dogs like that. I wouldn't have dared."

"You saved us," Annalie said. "Thank you."

Blossom looked into Annalie's eyes, and for the first time saw something like respect there. A confused but happy feeling rose up in her; of all the crew of the *Sunfish*, Annalie was the one she had most wanted to impress.

"How did you set the branches on fire?" Essie asked curiously.

Blossom produced a box of matches from her pocket. "They're from the cruise ship. And no, I *didn't* steal them."

Will laughed. "It's good to be prepared."

"You should have seen her," Annalie said approvingly. "She was *terrifying*."

Blossom basked in the sudden warm glow of their approval.

Watching her, Pod felt something relax inside himself, the tight anxious feeling he'd been carrying around since the day he brought her aboard: the fear that this was all going to go wrong; that she'd never find a place among his friends; that one day he'd have to choose between them. Because of course it wouldn't be a choice—he'd have to go with his sister—but he'd dreaded the thought of losing the best friends he'd ever had.

Now he thought maybe it was all going to work out after all.

Surfing the desert

Surfing a desert was both like and unlike sailing the seas.

The red desert was both sandy and stony, and as they went deeper into it, they found themselves rising and falling over dunes that were a little like an ocean swell. The sun beat down on them just as it frequently did at sea. And the wind turned out to be fickle and temperamental, gusting and fading according to its own whims, so that sometimes they sailed along quite smartly, but at other times they barely moved at all.

It wasn't long before the cool ocean breezes faded away entirely and they were in a hot country that was staggeringly dry. The temperature rose and rose and rose. There was no shade to be seen anywhere. The water they'd brought with them began to seem pitifully small.

"I really wish we could have waited till nightfall," Will grumbled as the wind dropped for the umpteenth time and the surfer slowed to a crawl. "The sun's unbelievable."

"Maybe we should stop," Annalie suggested. "Use the sail as an awning. Try and get some rest and wait until it gets dark before we start again."

"It won't give us much shade," Will said. "We're better off trying to get there as quick as we can. Apart from anything else, we know Beckett's still out there somewhere. We need to get to Spinner first."

Annalie turned to Essie. "You got any signal yet?"

They'd both brought their shells with them in the hope that, somewhere on this remote shore, they might be able to send a message to Spinner. Fortunately, Essie had suggested they seal them inside a waterproof bag, so they'd survived their dunking in the waters of Kinle Bay. But when she checked her shell now there was no signal.

They surfed on. As they traveled, Will began to realize there was one very significant difference between sailing on water and surfing on land. The desert was both gritty and stony, and the further they went, the more the sand and stones chipped away at the wheels, worked their way into the axles and ground into the mechanism that kept them moving forward. Gradually, slowly, the wheels began to seize. The ride grew bumpier, until at last the wheels wouldn't turn at all.

"Everybody off," Will sighed.

They stood there in the blazing sun while Will tipped the surfer over for a look.

"This might take some work," he said grimly.

Pod and Annalie turned the sail into a makeshift shelter, but the sand was so hot that they couldn't sit on it. They crouched in the meager shade, sweating, while Will worked on the surfer's undercarriage, swearing intermittently.

"How far away do you think we are?" Pod asked Annalie.

"It's difficult to tell," Annalie admitted. "We're on the right heading. But I don't know how much further we've got to go."

"Is it a day? Two days?"

Annalie shrugged helplessly.

An hour passed. Will was still working on the surfer.

"I'm thirsty," Blossom said.

"We're all thirsty," Pod said. "We have to preserve our water."

"Maybe we should all have a sip," Essie said.

"I'm thirstier than that," Blossom said.

"No kidding," Will snarled from underneath an axle.

Trying to help, Essie turned to Annalie. "Could we try and make a solar still, like we did back on the island?"

"We didn't bring any plastic," Annalie said, "and the air and the ground are so dry I don't think we'd get any water anyway. Let's see exactly how much water we've got."

They had four full water bottles, each of them holding about a liter of water. There were five of them plus Graham; the water wouldn't last for long in this fierce heat. Annalie carefully poured water out for each of them and they drank, savoring it as much as they could, wishing they could have more.

Another hour passed. Eventually, Will said, "Okay, I might have fixed it."

179

He put the sail back on the surfer and they all climbed aboard. They sailed on bumpily. As the sun moved to the west, a wind came up and began to blow steadily. They started to make better time, although the wheels felt jerkier than before. They came to a rocky, eroded part of the country, and then, quite suddenly, Will swung the sail and brought them to an abrupt halt that threw Pod right out of the surfer.

"Careful," he said grumpily, picking grit out of his palms. Then he looked up and realized why Will had stopped them so abruptly.

They had arrived at a canyon. It was wide— perhaps several hundred yards across—and stretched out across their paths in both directions, a great rift across the middle of the desert.

"This was *not* on the map," Essie said.

They crept to the edge and looked down. The inside of the canyon was not a cliff: it was sloping and steep, but not vertical, made of huge rocks and patches of gritty sand and gravel. It was very deep—so deep they could not see the bottom clearly.

"So now what?" said Will.

"Do we try and go around it?" Essie suggested.

"It looks like it goes for miles," Annalie said. "Are you *sure* it's not on the map?"

Essie checked her shell, and shook her head.

"Weird," Annalie said. "So we've got no idea how big this thing is or how far it goes."

"We could end up going miles out of our way if we try to go around it," Will said.

"So, what? Are we going to climb down it?" Pod asked, looking uneasily at the drop.

"I don't think we've got a choice," Will said.

"I can't climb down there," Blossom said decisively.

"It's not climbing," Will said. "It's just very careful walking. You'll be fine. We'll all be fine."

"What happens when we get to the other side?" Essie asked. "Without the land surfer, we'll be walking the rest of the way."

The heat shivered over them. No one liked the sound of this very much.

Will looked down at the canyon, chewing his lip, then looked at the surfer. "We'll take it with us," he said.

"That's impossible!" Annalie said.

The land surfer could of course be broken down into components—that was how they'd brought it to shore—but they were big and unwieldy. To climb down the canyon and then climb up the other side, they would need to use both hands and all their strength.

"No it's not," Will said. "I'll take the sail, that's the heaviest part. The rest of you can take the other bits. We'll divide it up; it won't be that hard. Come on—we've got hardly any water. Do you really want to spend the next two days walking through this?"

They were all silent for a moment, looking at each other. Then Pod said, "Let's take this thing apart then."

"We're doing this? Really?" Blossom said.

"We can't stay here," Pod sighed.

Will set to work pulling his land surfer apart, then he used what little rope they had to tie the biggest

181

pieces onto his, Pod's, and Annalie's backs. Essie took one of the backpacks, loaded up with the remaining bits and pieces of the land surfer, while Blossom was given the other, filled with food and water.

"Okay," Will said when everybody was fully loaded. "Let's do this."

He led the way, picking a path through the rocks and down into the canyon. They discovered very quickly that the ground between the rocks was treacherous—the surface was loose and slipped easily. "It's safer if you climb down over the rocks," Will called after his feet nearly went out from under him for the second time. He picked his way cautiously down; Will was sure-footed and would have had no trouble descending ordinarily, but the big sail on his back kept catching on things, startling him, and it was so heavy it threw his balance off, so he was constantly in fear he was going to fall.

They inched their way down, Annalie following Will, Essie behind them, and Pod in the rear with Blossom. Blossom had no special aptitude for climbing and kept having to be told where to put her hands and feet. It made for slow going. Pod, weighed down by the land surfer's heavy axles, grew more and more tired.

They were almost two-thirds of the way to the bottom when Essie's feet went out from under her. She squealed and skidded and loose rocks began to cascade down over Annalie and Will, who were downhill from her. She managed to catch herself in time, but her sudden cry had spooked everyone else; Blossom lost her grip on the rock she was climbing and began to fall. Pod grabbed for her, but missed. Blossom began to slide, finding a chute of bare scree that whisked her down the slope, past Essie, past Annalie, and then directly into Will. She smacked into him and then the two of them smacked into a rock, which stopped their headlong slide with a terrifying crunch.

For a long moment, neither of them moved. Essie, Pod, and Annalie skittered down to them as quickly as they dared, terrified.

"Blossom? Will? Are you all right?" Pod said.

As they reached them they both stirred, groaning. Blossom levered herself off Will. Will peeled himself off the rock.

"Ow," he said, feeling his ribs, then his head. A big egg-shaped lump was already coming up through his hair.

"Have you broken anything? Is it serious?" Annalie asked.

They'd all heard something crunch in the impact.

Will moved his limbs, testing them out carefully. He'd fallen on one arm, and it was very tender but not agonizing. "Nope. Nothing broken."

"Blossom," Pod said, "what about you? Can you walk?"

Blossom examined herself, and found a long scrape down her leg and the side of her body where she'd scoured the skin away in her slide. "That really hurts," she said.

"But is anything broken or sprained?" Pod insisted.

Blossom shook her head, still dazed.

"Will," Annalie said. "The sail."

The mast had been smashed by the impact, and the sail itself, which had been neatly furled, now had a long jagged tear in it.

"We might be able to fix it," Pod said, not very convincingly.

Will looked back over his shoulder at the sail, grim-faced. "Maybe," he said.

"Sorry," Blossom said in a small voice.

"Let's keep going," Will said, his voice tight. "And this time, everybody be more careful."

They climbed down to the bottom of the canyon without further mishap. When they reached the bottom, Essie said, "I think we could all do with another drink and something to eat."

Blossom took off her backpack and handed it over.

Essie opened it, and said, "Hey, why is this—?"

Then a look of horror came over her face.

A water bottle had broken open inside the bag. All that precious water had been wasted, spilled into the bag, and worse, it had soaked into their remaining food. She pulled the sopping wet food out in dismay.

"Our food ruined, too?" Will said furiously.

"No, not ruined," Essie said gamely. "It's just a bit wet, but that's okay, we can eat and drink at the same time. Here, I'll divide it up."

They made the best of their soggy food and ate it sitting in the rocky bottom of the canyon. Will finished first and sat for a while with the broken pieces of the sail, trying to think of a way to fix it. But they had no tools and no spares, and the rocky canyon bottom contained nothing he could use to splint his mast or sew up the ripped sail.

"Maybe we could ..." Pod began, wanting to help, but couldn't think of anything else to say.

Will looked at it for a few minutes longer, then said, "Forget it. There's nothing to be done."

Annalie looked at him, then at Essie. "I guess we're walking then."

They rested for a little longer, then began their ascent, leaving the abandoned pieces of the land surfer lying at the bottom of the canyon; there seemed no point carrying them any further, and as a result, the climb up was a lot easier than the climb down had been.

Traversing the canyon had swallowed up most of the afternoon. They walked now with the sun behind them, casting shadows in front of them that grew longer and longer. As the sun sank, the blazing heat faded; the temperature plummeted. None of them had planned for this; no one had brought warm clothes. They began to shiver.

"We won't be so cold if we keep moving," Annalie said.

It was cold and weary walking, the sand sifting into their shoes, stones turning under their feet. When, later, the moon rose, it was easier to see where they were going, but all it revealed was a vast expanse of nothingness.

"Maybe we should stop and make camp for the night," Essie suggested. "Blossom's got matches. We could light a fire."

"No firewood," Will growled.

"Oh. Good point," Essie said.

They kept walking. Annalie was in front, leading them with the compass. The compass points glowed in the dark, but even so, it was hard to read, and she began to feel that her world had narrowed to the stony ground under her feet and the wobbling green arrow that floated in front of her eyes.

Hours passed. The stars blazed cold and beautiful in the desert sky. They stumbled on, exhausted, thirsty, hungry.

Suddenly, a welcome sound: Essie's shell pinged.

"Signal!" she gasped, whipping it out.

Annalie took out her own shell. She'd written a message to Spinner as they were entering Kinle Bay; now it flew off into the night: *Spinner, we're here in Sundia. We're coming to see you. Please wait for us. Reply as soon as you get this message.* Prompted by Will, she'd added a second message: *Beckett is following us. Be careful!!*

"If there's signal, that must mean we're close to a settlement," Will said.

"Maybe it's the Ark!" Essie said.

"I hope so," Annalie said.

They waited for several minutes, but no answer to their messages came. "Do we keep going?" Annalie asked finally.

"I guess so," Will said.

They kept walking. They walked for what seemed like a long time.

"Where's the Ark?" Essie asked. "Shouldn't we be able to see it by now?"

Annalie said nothing. A nasty worried feeling was creeping over her. "Do you still have signal?" she asked.

They took their shells out.

Nothing.

"Does that mean we've overshot?" Will asked.

"Are we lost?" Pod asked, his voice wobbling.

"It'll be okay," Annalie said gamely. "When the sun comes up, I can work out where we are."

"We should go back where there's signal," Essie said. "Tell them to come and get us."

"We don't even know where that is. We could be walking in circles," Pod said.

"We *haven't* been walking in circles!" Annalie said fiercely, but before anyone else could respond, Graham spoke up. "Something coming."

"Oh, what now?" Essie moaned. "Giant man-eating desert lizards?"

They drew closer together, afraid that Sundia was about to throw some new danger their way.

"There!" Blossom pointed.

A wavering, sinister shape was silhouetted on the top of a dune, long-legged and impossibly tall. For a moment it seemed their worst fears had been realized; then Annalie said, "Is that someone on a camel?"

The camel galloped down the dune and began coming toward them; a second and a third followed.

"Should we be running toward them, or away, do you think?" Will said warily, remembering that Sundians liked to throw foreigners in prison.

"Too late now," Annalie said. "They've seen us."

None of them had the energy to run any further. Cold, exhausted, thirsty, they stood and watched in resignation as the camel train came toward them.

The lead rider drew up in front of them. The camel kneeled. A slight figure stepped lightly from the saddle and said, "Which one of you is Annalie?" It was a woman's voice.

Hope flared in all their hearts. Annalie stepped forward. "I am."

"I'm Sola—Sola Prentice. How did you get out here?"

"It's a long story," Annalie said.

"You can tell us back at the Ark," Sola said. "I've got someone here who's been dying to see you."

As she spoke, the second camel kneeled and they saw its rider step down onto the sand, his parrot's crest of silver hair shining in the moonlight.

"Spinner!" Annalie cried. She and Will launched themselves into his arms, almost knocking him sideways.

"Steady on!" he said, laughing, hugging them to him as tight as could be, and for a few long minutes they were all hugs and laughter. Graham spiraled above them, letting out huge ripping shrieks, before he sailed down to land on Spinner's shoulder.

"Bad Spinner," Graham said. "Spinner went away."

"I know," Spinner said, stroking him. "I didn't want to. But it had to be done."

"You're lucky we found you," Sola said. "There's a lot of desert out here to get lost in."

"*She* said we weren't lost," Will said, poking Annalie.

"We weren't," Annalie said.

Spinner smiled. "Let's get you back to the Ark."

The Ark

The rest of the journey was something of a blur. Camels were produced for all of them, and they lurched through the night, lulled into a half-doze by the animals' rolling gait. The Ark, when they reached it, appeared little more than a huge dark shape rising out of the desert before they were whisked inside, and found drinks and food and beds, where they all collapsed into desperate slumber.

The next morning, they were all awake within minutes of each other. They were in a bunkroom, clean, tidy, utilitarian, but windowless.

Spinner soon appeared in the doorway.

"We didn't get a chance to do proper introductions last night," he said, giving a twinkly-eyed smile to Essie, Pod and Blossom. "I'm Spinner."

"I'm Essie Wan. Me and Annalie met at school."

"I'm Pod. These guys rescued me. This is my sister Blossom."

"I'm new," Blossom said.

Spinner laughed, then turned to Will and Annalie, trying to look stern. "I've got a bone to pick with you two. What are you doing in Sundia?

I thought I told you to go home. You promised me you'd go home."

"We promised we'd stay safe," Annalie said.

"Not that we'd go home," Will said. "It's different."

"It doesn't sound like you managed that either," Spinner said. "I get to Sundia and my shell's full of messages about kidnappers and ransoms."

"*You* were the one who went to Brundisi," Will said. "We only went there because we were following you."

Spinner gave them a squinty-eyed look. "All right, well, don't make a habit of it. From now on, you do what I say, right?"

Will and Annalie looked at each other and giggled.

"You think I'm kidding?" Spinner said, but didn't follow through on the threat. "Who wants some breakfast?"

Spinner took them to the Ark canteen, which had an extensive breakfast menu. Sola soon joined them and encouraged them to order whatever they liked. Will ordered everything.

"Are we allowed to be here?" Annalie asked, looking nervously at the other people in the canteen. They were the first Sundians they'd seen; the ones in the canteen had bronze-brown skin, dark hair and eyes, and, like their gods, were mostly built on a monumental scale. Some of them had nodded and smiled at the children when they came in; none of them seemed particularly troubled that they were there.

"It's fine," Sola said. "They know you're with me." She paused, then added, "The Ark isn't like the rest of Sundia. Anywhere else, you'd probably be arrested—there are big rewards for anyone who catches a foreigner. But this is still an international research station, at least in theory. We don't mind the odd foreigner here."

"So are you Sundian?" Annalie asked.

"Half Sundian," Sola said. She was slight and smiley, with big dark eyes and a sweep of long straight dark hair. "I was born and raised in Dux, but my mother was born here, and I still have family here. When we all went on the run, this seemed like the obvious place to come. My cousin works here and she got me a job— first as a gardener, which was fun, actually. But then they found out what I could actually do—"

"What's that?"

"Advanced computer system engineering. So now I work in operations keeping the Ark going."

"What *is* the Ark anyway?" Essie asked.

"After breakfast, I'll give you the tour," Spinner said.

Their food arrived, and for a while, no one said anything. When the eating finally slowed, Spinner said, "So tell me, what's this about an Admiralty ship following you?"

"It's the same one that came after you in Dio," Will said. "I recognized it straight away."

"An Admiralty ship can't be here," Sola said. "They wouldn't dare enter Sundian waters."

"This one did," Will said.

"And you think they're following you?" Spinner asked.

192

"It sure looked like it," Annalie said.

Spinner turned to Sola. "Then we need an exit strategy."

"I'm on it," Sola said, and got to her feet.

"Will we get to go on a pirate submarine?" Will asked hopefully.

"You don't want to go on a pirate submarine," Spinner said. "Trust me."

"Why not?" asked Will.

"Imagine climbing inside a noisy hot tin can with a bunch of smelly pirates, then going to the bottom of the ocean and staying down there for weeks."

"Right," Will said, deciding that perhaps submarines were not so cool after all.

"Where are we going to go?" Annalie asked. "After this?"

Spinner sighed. "That's a very good question. We can't go home—even if Beckett's guys hadn't wrecked it, I'm sure they're still watching the place."

"We could find a new home, couldn't we?" Will suggested. "I mean for all of us."

"I have a home," Essie said quickly. "But Pod and Blossom don't."

"Well, you're very welcome to stick with me," Spinner said kindly, "if that's what you want to do. But I can't promise you it's going to be very comfortable. I've been on the run for months now, and there's no sign that that's going to change anytime soon."

"We've got a place," Will said eagerly. "We found it. There's an island, back in the Moon Islands. Me and Essie got marooned there, which kind of sucked, but it has this castle on it! And it's deserted! And it would make an awesome hideout!"

"It wouldn't take much work to fix it up," Essie added. "You'd need to bring in some power—and some food—"

"But there's loads of space for everyone, and it's quiet and secluded. It'd be a red-hot hideout," Will said.

Spinner raised his eyebrows. "Sounds intriguing. There are worse places to hide than the Moon Islands—as you know. But first we've got to get away from Sundia. And that might take some doing."

"The *Sunfish* is anchored in Kinle Bay," Will said. "We can just go. Right now."

"We might need some help chasing off that whale," Pod said.

"What whale?"

"Bad fish," Graham said disapprovingly. "Big teeth."

Quickly they told Spinner the story of their action-packed journey to shore. Spinner listened in astonishment. "Feral dogs and temple whales? I'm amazed you made it here at all."

"You really think it was a temple whale?" asked Annalie.

"Must have been. I didn't think there were any left."

Blossom looked at Will triumphantly. Will ignored her. "So why don't we just go?" he said. "Get away before Beckett finds us."

194

Spinner shook his head. "We'll need some help organizing safe passage, otherwise we could end up with the Sundian coastguard to deal with. And that could be even worse than the Admiralty."

He looked around at the empty plates. "All finished? Who'd like a tour of the Ark?"

By daylight, the Ark rose up out of the desert with the vast heft of an ancient monument. But this one hadn't been hewn from stone. It was a massive structure built with the strongest reinforced concrete, and it dated back to the time before the Flood. In those years, as the climate went dangerously out of control, ecosystems started collapsing and hundreds of species began to go extinct. A coalition of national governments, charities, and some absurdly rich private investors had come together to build the Ark. It was a facility designed to house both living and preserved specimens of every kind of life: not just animals, but insects and plants, too. The Sundian desert had been chosen because it was geologically and climatically stable, and also extremely remote. Although the Sundians had not yet withdrawn into isolation at the time the Ark was built, there was already a strong religious element in its government, and they agreed to accept the Ark on Sundian soil for religious reasons, rather than from a spirit of international cooperation. They believed that the sea god had risen from the cradle of life in the sea to create the land and everything on it, scattering himself across the world in multiple forms—male and female, plant and insect, mammal and reptile. That meant that protecting this creation was not just a practical imperative, it was a religious duty. So while the Ark was certainly a research station, to the Sundians it was also a kind of temple.

Above ground, the Ark contained a series of sky-lit galleries the size of football stadiums filled with trees and flowers, animals and birds, frogs and insects: mini ecosystems with their own climate-controlled environments, supported by a network of plant nurseries and animal breeding areas and insect hatcheries.

Spinner walked them past the huge spaces, letting them marvel at the sight of living things they had never glimpsed before. They saw deserts and rainforests, grasslands and forests, all filled root to tip with life.

"This place is like the world's most amazing zoo," Essie said.

"It's just a tiny sliver of what the world used to contain," Spinner said. "But it's something."

The soaring concrete galleries above the ground were only a part of the Ark. The complex extended deep underground as well. The first level below ground was the living quarters for the Ark's extensive staff: the gardeners and botanists, veterinarians and animal breeders and scientists, maintenance and tradespeople, cooks and cleaners and medics. There were enough people living and working in the Ark to fill a small town. Below that, occupying another three levels, was an enormous archive. The archive was almost unimaginably vast. It contained everything from ancient ice cores to seed banks to cryogenically preserved specimens, as well as truly vast amounts of research data housed on servers that stretched for miles. It had been built to be self-sustaining and self-preserving, using all the very best long-term technology, in the hope that at some point in the future, some of these forms of life could be returned to the world.

Spinner took them down in a lift that seemed to take a very long time to travel between one level and the next. They stepped out into the cool darkness of the archive; as the elevator doors opened, lights flicked on directly in front of them, hinting at many corridors, but the vast majority of the cavernous space they could sense around them was entirely dark and humming quietly.

"What's wrong with the lights?" Essie asked.

"Most of the time there's nobody down here," Spinner explained. "They have motion sensors that switch the lights on where you need them, and after a while they switch off again."

Will tested them, making little darting runs into the darkness to see how quickly he could make the lights come on, crowing with delight. They began to walk past rows and rows of corridors stretching away into the distance. Some were lined with cupboards and drawers, others with rows of fridges or freezers.

"What is all this stuff?" Annalie asked.

"A record of life on our world," Spinner said. "Specimens, samples, genetic material."

"You mean extinct things?"

"They have a lot of seeds, and the plants could certainly be brought back and propagated. But a lot of the specimens down here are extinct, yes. When this place was first set up, they hoped they might be able to bring some of them back one day."

"Is that possible?" asked Will.

"Before the Flood, I think they were getting close, technologically. These days, I doubt it," Spinner said. "Hopefully, one day, smarter people than us will be able to do something with all this knowledge."

"Look at this row," Annalie said. "It looks really old."

It was a long row of antique cupboards, lockers and drawers, the wood glowing from years of furniture polish.

"It *is* old," Spinner said. "This used to be a museum collection. They donated it to the Ark. Collections like these take up a lot of room and they're expensive to maintain, so I guess the museum was happy to get rid of it."

"Collections of what?" asked Pod.

Spinner checked the labels, which were handwritten in a beautiful script on cards which were beginning to brown. The scientific names were incomprehensible to the children. He pulled open a drawer. Five little furry animals lay inside, looking very dead and a little deflated.

"The Lesser Duxan Ground Squirrel," Spinner said. "Extinct for about a hundred years."

"Why do they look like that?" asked Pod. "Kind of weird."

"They're museum specimens," Spinner said. "They were preserved and stuffed. All that's left are the skins."

"They were cute," Essie said wistfully.

"After they introduced foxes to Dux, they didn't stand a chance," Spinner said.

"Are all these drawers and cupboards full of dead things?" Pod asked.

"More or less," Spinner said.

"Hey, check this out!"

Blossom had wandered off and opened another drawer, further down on the other side. Now she was beckoning to them excitedly.

They all came to see what she'd found. Spinner caught his breath, and Graham let out a horrified squawk.

There in the drawer were six birds who looked almost exactly like Graham, along with a smaller juvenile and some eggs.

Graham flapped agitatedly around and then landed on Spinner's shoulder. "Who did this?" he rasped.

"It happened a long time ago," Spinner said softly. He read the notes on the cards accompanying each specimen. "Some of these are more than a hundred years old."

Graham peered at the birds suspiciously. "How they die?"

"I don't know. Caught by collectors? They may have just died of old age."

Graham whistled thoughtfully.

"If they've got them here, does that mean ..." Annalie began.

199

She stopped before she could finish the thought, but Graham caught her drift.

"Graham not extinct!" he snapped.

"Of course you're not," Spinner said soothingly. "You're an exceptional bird."

Pod glared at Blossom. "Why did you have to show him?" he hissed.

Blossom was baffled by his anger. "I thought it was cool."

"They're his ancestors," Pod said. "Dead and stuffed. How would you like it?"

"Do you think there are ghosts down here?" Blossom said. She didn't look frightened; if anything, she looked a little excited. "With all these dead things, I bet there are heaps of ghosts."

Essie shuddered. "This place is creepy," she said, turning to the others. "Can we go?"

The sight of the dead parrots had thrown a pall over all of them, and they were happy to leave the dark and labyrinthine corridors of the archives behind. Down there, everything was already dead and gone, a memory of all that had been lost; up above, it felt like there was still hope, for there everything was still alive and thriving.

When they reached the habitat level, they all went their separate ways, in search of lunch (Will and Pod), a long, hot shower (Essie), and undisclosed business (Blossom). Annalie lingered with Spinner.

"There's something I need to tell you," she said. "I found the memory stick."

"Oh." Spinner looked at her warily.

"When I ran away from school, I took Lolly with me. I don't know why, I just … Anyway, I still had her when we landed at Uncle Art's place. His kids broke her and the memory stick fell out."

"And then what happened to it?"

"I got it back and we left. But Uncle Art saw the stick, and he knows I've got it. He was working for the Admiralty the whole time, Spinner. He must have told them I have it."

"So they got to Art?" Spinner sighed. "I can't blame him, I guess. They would've made it pretty tough for him."

Annalie couldn't understand why Spinner wasn't angrier. "He betrayed you. He betrayed all of us!"

"He's got a family of his own to consider," Spinner said. He looked at her sadly. "I'm sorry you got caught up in all this. I should have done more to keep you safe. I thought you *were* safe. I was wrong."

"It's all right," Annalie said. "We can look after ourselves."

Spinner gave her an affectionate look. "You and your brother are the smartest, toughest kids on the planet. I'm lucky to have you." He paused. "So where is the memory stick now?"

"It's right here."

Through all their adventures she had kept the memory stick safe, secured inside several layers of waterproofing, and then stitched into a secret pocket of her shorts. Now she gave it to Spinner.

He sighed, looking down at the little object nestled in his hand.

"Did I do the wrong thing bringing it to you?" she asked anxiously.

"No," Spinner said, "you did the right thing."

"What are you going to do with it now?"

"I'm going to put it somewhere safe," Spinner said. "Thank you for looking after it."

Later that day, Annalie was lying on her bunk reading a book she'd found in the canteen. Essie came in, clean, pressed, and smelling of conditioner, her hair a shiny miracle.

"You smell nice," Annalie said. "Is it good to be clean again?"

"It's heaven," Essie said. "Did you know they have a hairdresser here on staff? She gave me a trim."

"Oh, so she did," Annalie said. She was not very tuned in to details of personal grooming. "It looks nice."

"Thanks," Essie said. But she had not really come to talk about hair. She had more pressing things on her mind. "Can I talk to you about something?"

Annalie looked at her curiously, then put her book aside. "Of course."

"We always said," Essie said slowly, "that this journey was about finding Spinner. Right?"

"Right," Annalie said.

"And I was glad to come. I've loved it—mostly— except for the bad bits. I could've done without getting shipwrecked and then nearly starving to death on the raft. But this has been the most amazing adventure."

"We couldn't have done it without you," Annalie said.

"The thing is ... I've been thinking ..." Essie said, coming to the crux of what she wanted to say. "Now that we *have* found Spinner ..."

"Oh," Annalie said, suddenly realizing what Essie was getting at. "You want to go home."

Essie was stricken by the look of sudden disappointment on Annalie's face. "It doesn't have to be straight away. I mean, I know we're still a long way from Dux. I just ... it's been so long now and ... When I finally got to message my dad, I realized how much I missed him."

Essie's eyes were welling up as she blurted out her feelings. Seeing this, Annalie began to get teary too. "Oh, don't cry!" she said. "Of course you have to go home. We've been so selfish, dragging you all the way around the world like this. It's time we let you go home."

"You don't mind?" Essie said.

"Of course I *mind*," Annalie said. "I'm going to miss you heaps. I've never had a friend like you."

"I've never had a friend like you, either," Essie said, gulping back tears.

"But you're right. It's time. Send him a message. Tell him you're coming home."

"Are you sure?" Essie asked.

"Of course I'm sure," Annalie said. "Sola's working on a plan to get us home. I don't know when it's going to happen exactly, but with a bit of luck, we're probably only a few weeks away from Dux."

Essie smiled, filled with a mixture of joy, relief, and sadness. "Shall I message him now?"

"Yes! Right now! Why not?"

Essie sat down on her own bunk and began to type a message into My Monster. The message went off with a growl. To her surprise, moments later, her shell began to ring.

She looked at the caller ID and squeaked with surprise. "Dad, is that you?"

"Essie! It's so good to hear your voice! Where are you, are you all right?"

"I'm fine, but what about you? How come you can call me? I thought they were monitoring your calls?"

"That's all over. I'm free."

"What do you mean?"

"The trial. It's over, and they set me free."

"I knew you were innocent!" Essie cried. "Oh Dad, that's so amazing! I can't believe it!"

"I'm not exactly innocent," her father said sadly. "I was found not guilty of the charges laid against me, but as a company we've got a lot to answer for. Things are going to change at Tower Corp, you can count on that. But that's not something for you to worry about. The good news is, I'm a free man again. But you still haven't told me where you are."

"I'm not sure if I should say," Essie said. "That's sort of what I wanted to talk to you about. Our mission is over now—well, pretty much—and I'm ready to come home."

Her dad gave a happy sigh. "Thank goodness! I'll come and get you myself."

"You don't have to do that. We're coming home very soon." Essie paused. "What happened about the house? Did we lose the house?"

"The house? Well. That's a little complicated. But don't worry—there'll always be a place for you, even if it's not quite as grand as you're used to."

"I don't care about grand," Essie said. "I just want to see you."

"Same here, darling," Essie's dad said, his voice sounding a little choked. "I won't hound you about where you are. But can you promise me you're somewhere safe?"

Essie pulled a face. *Was* she somewhere safe? She wasn't entirely sure. "Safe enough, I think," she said.

"And what happened to your friend, the one who was kidnapped by pirates? Did you get her back?"

"Oh yes," Essie said. "She managed to escape all by herself. We didn't need the ransom money in the end."

"So where is it now?"

"Oh, I've still got it," Essie said, feeling slightly embarrassed. "I can give it back to you."

"Maybe you should hang onto it, in case something else comes up." He paused. "You know, whatever trouble your friends are in, I might be able to help. You know I've got great lawyers."

Essie hesitated, attracted by the thought of getting some high-powered help. "It's a good idea, Dad. I'll talk to the others."

"I have to go," her father said. "But stay in touch, okay? Don't disappear on me."

205

"Okay."

"I love you, Essie. I can't wait to see you again."

"I love you, too," Essie said.

"I'll see you soon," her father said, and ended the call.

Essie sat there for a moment, a feeling of giddy relief washing over her. In the space of a few moments, it felt like all her troubles and worries and fears had been swept away. Her journey was over, her father was free (not exonerated exactly, but free), and now she could go home. It had been so wonderful to hear her father's voice again, and it had brought with it a sharp, yearning desire for home. There had been plenty of moments when she had wished herself out of danger and far away, but this was almost the first time she had allowed herself to fully admit how much she longed for the safety and security of home, to be protected and comforted and looked after and loved.

"Is everything okay?" Annalie asked. Of course, she had heard the whole conversation.

Essie nodded, her eyes shimmering. "It'll be good to go home again," she said.

Exit strategy

Essie shared her news with the others over dinner in the canteen.

"Like rats deserting a sinking ship," Will joked. "You're the first rat."

"This ship isn't sinking," Spinner put in.

"You can come and visit me," Essie said. Now that her heart was set on departure, she was already starting to miss her friends.

"So what about the rest of us?" Annalie asked. "Do we know where we're going?"

Spinner scrunched his face up. "I have a few ideas," he said. "Right now, I'm keeping it loose."

"Do we have to have a destination?" Will asked. "Couldn't we just keep sailing?"

"*We're* going to Violeta," Blossom said.

The others looked at her, surprised.

"Why there?" Spinner asked curiously.

"It has castles and palaces and cakes. It's the best place in the whole world."

"How do you know?" Pod asked.

"The destination book. On the ship every cabin had one. It told you about every place we stopped so the passengers would know whether they wanted to get off the boat and visit."

"Could you read the destination book?" Pod asked, surprised.

"No. It had pictures."

"Violeta's a beautiful city," Spinner said.

"Good biscuits," Graham added, nodding.

"But it's expensive. And it's a very ... bureaucratic sort of place."

"What does that mean?" Pod asked.

"If you don't have papers, it'd be very difficult to find work or a place to live," Spinner explained. "They certainly wouldn't let you go to school there."

"Fine by me," Blossom said, meaning school.

"Is it like Norlind?" Pod asked fearfully. "They're very sticky about papers there."

"Most of the Northlands are pretty sticky about papers," Spinner said.

Blossom could tell which way the wind was blowing. "You promised we could go to Violeta," she said accusingly to Pod.

"I know, but ..."

"We can *go* to Violeta," Spinner said. "Eventually. But you can't live there. I'm sorry."

Blossom scowled.

Sola came to join them. "Our exit strategy's all organized," she said. "At dawn tomorrow, a camel train will take you back across the desert to Kinle Bay. I put in a report to the mistress of the temple about the feral dogs. The religious people can be a bit slow to get going, but hopefully they will have

208

sent someone out there to chase them off. We're all Kinlemotukinle's creatures, but still, you can't have them terrorizing people in the temple grounds."

"What about the shadow whale?" asked Will.

"One of my cousins will meet us at the Bay. He knows how to handle the whale."

"He won't hurt it, will he?" asked Annalie.

"Of course not," Sola said, looking scandalized. "Then another one of my cousins will escort you out of Sundian waters. He knows a guy who knows a guy who can help you avoid the naval patrols and get you past the barrier without tripping it."

"Are there that many naval patrols really?" Will asked. "We didn't see a single Sundian ship when we were sailing down the coast."

"You got lucky, then," Sola said. "They're out there. And if they catch you, they'll throw you in jail forever."

"We'd better not let them catch us, then," Spinner said. He looked around at the kids. "Better get your gear together. We've got an early start in the morning."

It didn't take them long to pack. When they were finished, it still felt too early to go to bed. Essie and Annalie drifted up to the rooftop observation deck to look at the stars. The desert night was freezing, but this time they'd brought blankets.

Spinner and Sola were already there. "I'm going to miss this place," he said, reaching out to Annalie and tucking her under his arm. "You fell on your feet here, Sola."

"It's very special," Sola agreed. "It's hard to believe it still exists. But that's what it was built for."

"Are you coming with us when we go?" Annalie asked.

Sola shook her head with a smile. "There's nothing calling me back to Dux. I love my job and the work we're doing here. And even though I wasn't born here, I feel connected to Sundia. I can't imagine living anywhere else now. My mother always said—"

But they never had a chance to find out what Sola's mother always said, because a harsh voice suddenly cut through the night. "Hands up! You're under arrest by order of the Admiralty!"

Marines came pouring out the door, rifles trained on the four of them; still more came swarming up the outside of the Ark on ropes. They were surrounded.

"Hands up or I'll shoot!" barked the voice.

Spinner, Sola, Annalie and Essie put their hands up.

A man sauntered through the door and onto the observation deck, tall and barrel-chested, dressed in a leather jacket.

"I've been waiting a long time for this," said Beckett.

Putting the band
back together

"Hello, Beckett," said Spinner.

"Spinner. It's been a long time."

"Not long enough," said Spinner.

"You've got very enterprising kids," Beckett said, turning to look at Annalie. "Where's your brother?"

"The kids have nothing to do with this," Spinner said. "Your business is with me."

"That's not strictly true though, is it?" Beckett said. "She's got the research."

"No, I don't," Annalie said.

"Enough of the silly games," Beckett said impatiently. Quick as lightning, he grabbed Annalie; suddenly, there was a gun to her head. "One of you has it, and you're going to give it to me. Or the clever one dies."

"Don't give it to him!" Annalie cried.

Beckett's grip on her tightened. "Be quiet," he said. "The grown-ups are talking now."

"Let her go," Spinner said.

"I will," Beckett said. "As soon as you tell me where you've hidden the research."

For a long moment, the two of them glared at each other, old friends who were now the bitterest of enemies. Then Spinner let out a broken sigh. "All right," he said.

"No!" Annalie howled despairingly.

Sola put her face in her hands.

Beckett smiled triumphantly. "Cuff them all. Then my old friend Spinner can show us where he's hidden my research."

Will and Pod had snuck back into the canteen to look for a mid-evening snack. The canteen was now closed, but they hoped there might be something they could liberate from the fridge.

Just as Will opened the fridge door, an alarm started to blast.

"Whoa!" Will said, slamming it shut again. "Those Sundians really care about their food!"

"It's not just the canteen, it's everywhere," Pod said. "Something's wrong."

"Let's get out of here," Will said.

They scampered out of the kitchen and crossed the darkened dining room, heading for the door. Will heard movement outside; he grabbed Pod and the two of them ducked under a table.

Someone looked into the room, did a quick sweep, rifle at the ready, then, seeing nothing, moved on.

"Was that an Admiralty marine?" Will whispered.

"Sure looked like it," Pod said.

They looked at each other aghast.

As abruptly as it had started, the alarm switched off again.

"We've got to find the others," Will said.

Sola led the way to the control room, the operational heart of the Ark. The door was huge and heavy, like something on a submarine. "Open it," Beckett ordered.

"It's locked," Sola said. "When the alarm was triggered, the control center locked down automatically."

"Are you trying to tell me the chief engineer doesn't know how to override the lock?" Beckett said.

Sola looked at Spinner. "It's all right," he said.

Sola gave him a grave look, then entered the sequence that would override the security and unlock the door. It swung open.

There were three Sundians on duty inside. "Sola, thank goodness!" one of them said as Sola stepped into the room. "We got a report of intruders, but—"

The Sundian broke off as he saw the marines pushing in behind her.

"You. Out. Now," Beckett said.

With guns pointed at their heads, the Sundians had little choice but to do as he said.

"Lock that door," Beckett said when they were gone. "I don't want any surprises. Now. What have you brought me here to see?"

"Show him," Spinner said.

In the center of the control room was a large empty space. Sola went to a control panel at one edge of the space and tapped and swiped some commands. A huge three-dimensional display appeared. It showed a complex network represented by jewels of light strung on a vast system of glowing lines, different sections in different colors, as complex as a brain or a galaxy.

"What are we looking at?" Beckett asked.

"This is the Ark," Sola said. "Every system, every function, all the data."

Beckett studied it. "And why," he said, "should I care about that?"

"The research is there inside it," Spinner said.

"Yours and Sola's?"

"Vesh's too."

Beckett smiled. "You know I've already got Sujana and Dan's research, don't you? Sujana's seen the error of her ways. After all this is done, I'm going to set her up with a new job back in Pallas. Important work, good money. She'll be able to take proper care of her mother."

"I don't believe it," Sola said. "Why would she agree to go back?"

"She's had plenty of time to think about it," Beckett said. "And she always did believe the work was important."

"You threatened her mother," Spinner said.

"I didn't have to," Beckett said. "Once I'd explained it all to her properly, she was happy to come back."

"So, what," Sola said sarcastically, "you're putting the band back together?"

"I am," Beckett said. "You want to join? I could use you."

"Not in a million years," Sola said.

"What about me?" Spinner asked. "Am I invited back?"

"No," Beckett said icily. "I don't need you." He turned to Sola. "Show me the research."

"If you can find it, you're welcome to it," Sola said.

Beckett smiled. "I thought we were past this." He turned to one of his marines. "Shoot the girl."

The marine hesitated.

"Okay then, I will," Beckett said, and pointed a gun directly at the center of Annalie's forehead, cocking it ready to fire.

"Stop it!" Sola said, turning pale. She swiped and flicked, keyed in passwords, swiped and flicked again. The system moved and flashed, changed color, zoomed, and reconfigured itself until the network showed three webs of glowing color, distributed right through the huge whole.

Beckett put his gun away and walked right into the display, his face brilliantly lit by the glowing colors.

"Aha," Beckett said. "I want to see what's in those files."

"The files are encrypted," Spinner said. "They're all encrypted. You couldn't get Dan or Sujana's files to open, could you?"

Beckett's face flushed with anger, but then he smiled. "No," he said, "I couldn't. But now I've got the master key, haven't I? That's what your piece is. The key that unlocks all the doors."

"That's exactly what it is," Spinner said. "The key that unlocks the door to destruction. Forty years ago, the Collodius Device caused catastrophic changes to our world. We agreed back then that no one should have that kind of power ever again. Then, fifteen years ago, you started trying to rediscover those secrets."

"And you went along with it," Beckett said.

"We made a mistake," Sola said. "We thought some good could come out of understanding the process."

"But that's not why you wanted it," Spinner said. "You wanted a weapon. What were you thinking? Did you actually plan to use it? Or was it just there to threaten anyone who wouldn't fall into line? Be good or we'll send another Flood."

Beckett was shaking his head and chortling. "Still so paranoid. Why can't you accept that our motives were pure?"

"There's nothing pure about you, or your motives," Spinner said. "You and your cronies in the Admiralty would do anything to keep the world dependent on you. Keep us all believing the world's such a dangerous place we need a huge standing navy to keep us all safe. Safe from what? Pirates? Refugees?"

"Pirates are a genuine threat," Beckett said.

"Come on," Spinner said. "You know that's not true. The truth is, the Admiralty likes keeping everybody in a state of terror to justify their stranglehold on global politics."

Beckett gave a wolfish smile. "Now *that* is an exceptionally paranoid thing to say," he said. "But what do you think the governments of the world are likely to do if they ever find out that top-secret research into the Collodius Project was stolen from the Admiralty? What will they think, I wonder, when it's revealed that Dan Gari ended up as a leader of the Kang Brotherhood? And Vesh went to Brundisi, the country that started all this in the first place? Sola came to Sundia, which is an enemy of the new global alliance. And let's not forget *your* close ties to the Kang Brotherhood, Spinner." Beckett smiled. "It sounds bad, doesn't it? Like all the enemies of peace and prosperity are ganging up to make something terrible happen."

"It sounds like a delusional fantasy," Spinner said.

"It won't, though," Beckett said. "Not when I'm finished telling the story. Once everybody learns that the Sundians, the Brundisans and the pirates are conspiring to rebuild the Collodius Device, they'll be begging us to protect them."

Spinner shook his head in dismay. "It seems hard to believe we were ever friends," he said.

"The thing I find hard to understand is how you could live through the Flood," Beckett said, "and all the horrors that came after it, and not want to be sure you've got the strength to do something about it."

"Bring the Collodius Device back," Spinner said urgently, "and we could all be there again. And this time, there may not be anything left."

Beckett's eyes went dead. "I'm sick of talking about this," he said. "Time to see what all this fuss was about."

He reached into the inside pocket of his leather jacket and produced another memory chip, of more recent vintage than the one Annalie had brought with her. "Sujana and Dan Gari's work," he said, handing it to Sola. "Not the only copy, in case you were wondering. Plug it in."

Sola activated the chip, and with a great swirl, two new galaxies of light joined those of Spinner, Sola and Vesh.

"*Now* we're putting the band back together," Beckett said. "Let's open it."

"Don't do this," Spinner warned. "You'll regret it. I mean it."

"Open it," Beckett said.

Sola looked gravely at Spinner; he nodded. Sola took a deep breath and entered the command: decrypt.

Annalie watched in horror as connections began to spark between the lights, making new connections, reordering and reshaping, moving faster and faster; the secrets that had been kept safe for fifteen years were about to be revealed.

"It's working," Beckett said excitedly.

The five webs kept firing and connecting until they'd aligned themselves into a perfect, five-colored, glittering globe.

"Hmm," Beckett said, enjoying himself. "What shall I open first?"

He reached out to the interface and touched a light at random. For the briefest of moments, the display zoomed into the single light and revealed a directory, a branching list of file names. But then the first file name turned black and began to melt.

"What did you do?" Beckett yelled.

"I warned you not to open it," Spinner said.

As they watched, the effect began to spread.

Something was happening to the glittering five-colored globe: a change was spreading across it, breaking the connections; some lights were changing color, flaming out, turning black, disappearing; others grew huge and distorted and exploded in shimmers of sparks.

"What's happening?" Beckett said.

"A virus," Spinner said. "We built it into the encryption. If anyone else tried to bring the research together, it would immediately destroy itself. Permanently."

"They *were* the only copies of our research," Sola said. "In case you were wondering."

"How do you stop it?" Beckett demanded.

"It's too late," Spinner said. "Once it starts, it can't be stopped."

Beckett let out a roar of pure rage and lunged across the control room—not at Spinner, but at Annalie. In moments, he had her up against the wall with a gun at her head once more.

"Stop it!" he roared. "Or I'll kill her!"

"It can't be stopped!" Spinner shouted.

"It's already gone!" Sola said. "Look!"

The last points of light were going out, leaving only a diseased-looking, crumpled skeleton of broken connections. Beckett looked at it and saw that it was true. "Then I'll kill her anyway," he snarled.

Annalie heard the hammer pull back. She felt certain that these were her very last moments. She closed her eyes and squinched away from the cold metal of the gun.

"Stand down, sir."

Annalie opened her eyes in surprise. A marine was there, his rifle pointed at Beckett's head.

"You stay out of this," Beckett snarled.

"Sir, stand down, sir," the marine said again.

Annalie felt Beckett's muscles tighten—she felt a dreadful certainty that he was about to pull the trigger—and then Beckett released her. She staggered away from him.

"You think you've beaten me," Beckett snarled, his gun swinging wildly. "But no one gets the better of me."

The gun roared, deafening in the enclosed space. Annalie screamed. But then she realized Beckett had not fired at her. He had fired at Spinner.

And Spinner had collapsed to the floor.

An unexpected ally

Will and Pod crept toward their bunkroom. They had not seen any more marines since the first one, but they knew there must be more.

"How are we ever going to find the others?" Pod said. "This place is huge, and we don't know where to look."

"Essie'll have her shell," Will said. "I bet Annalie's left hers in the bunkroom. We can call her."

They walked into the bunkroom and saw Blossom, sitting cross-legged on her bunk, hide something under her pillow quick as a flash, then look at them with a smile of angelic innocence. Pod knew she must have been stealing things again, but there was no time to take her up on it.

"There are marines in the Ark," Pod said. "We need to find the others and get out of here."

Blossom's eyes widened and she quickly began gathering up her things.

Graham had been sleeping on a bunk rail, but the sound of their voices woke him up. "Admiralty? Here?"

"'Fraid so," Will said, digging about among Annalie's things. He pulled out her shell. "Found it!"

He was about to call Essie when Pod put out a warning hand.

"Don't," he said. "Someone might hear."

"Good point," Will said. He sent a message instead: *Where are you? The Admiralty are in the building, be careful!*

No reply came back.

"I guess we'd better go look for them," he said.

They gathered up their gear and ventured out to look for the others.

A Sundian man came hurrying past wearing gardening clothes and gumboots. Rather alarmingly, he was carrying a pitchfork.

"You kids, go back to your quarters," he warned. "We've been attacked, and it's not safe for you to be roaming around out here."

"What's happening? Where are they now?" asked Will.

"I heard they've taken the control room," the man said. "Now go on, back to your quarters, and stay out of the way until you hear the all-clear."

The man hurried away in the direction of the control room.

"We're following him, right?" Pod said.

"Of course," Will said.

"Spinner!" Annalie cried, running to his side.

Spinner was lying on the floor, blood already seeping from a wound in his side. His eyes were closed, and for a moment Annalie was afraid he might already be dead, but at the sound of her voice his eyes opened and he murmured, "You have to get out of here."

"We're not going anywhere without you," Annalie said.

"I'll be okay," Spinner said gamely. "I don't want you falling into his hands."

Sola shouted to the marines. "We need to get him to a doctor, now!"

The same marine who'd told Beckett to stand down crouched beside them. "How bad is it?" he asked.

"Bad," Sola said fearfully. "There's so much blood."

"You need to put pressure on the wound," the marine said. "Annalie, are you all right?"

For a split second she wondered how he knew her name, and then their eyes met and she realized that this was not just any Admiralty marine. It was Lieutenant Cherry.

"Sir," Cherry said, rising to his feet, "this man needs urgent medical attention."

"No one's going anywhere until I get what I want," Beckett said.

"What's left?" Sola cried bitterly. "You've got both of us. The research is gone. What more could you possibly want?"

"There are always more copies," Beckett said.

"No, there aren't," Sola said.

"She's telling the truth," Annalie said desperately. "Remember why Sujana got in touch with you?

223

She was afraid Spinner would destroy the research forever."

Beckett frowned. "He was bluffing."

"No, he wasn't," Annalie said. "He wouldn't bluff about something that important. He was ready to do anything to keep this research safe from you. Even if that meant destroying it."

Beckett looked from the defiant, frightened Annalie, to Sola, who was weeping now, angry and devastated. Finally, he grabbed Spinner by the shirt front and yanked him close. "Is that true? Is it gone?"

Spinner looked at him wearily and said, "It's finished, Avery."

Beckett stared at him for one long moment, then let out a roar of anger. He let Spinner slump to the ground.

"Arrest them all," he snarled. "Find the kids, too. And his stupid parrot."

"He needs medical attention," Cherry protested.

"And he'll get it," Beckett said, "when you've found the rest of the conspirators."

"No!" Sola cried.

"Sir, this is against the Admiralty code on the proper treatment of prisoners," Cherry said.

"I don't care what the code says," Beckett roared. "This is my operation and you will obey my commands or suffer the consequences."

"Sir, requesting permission to give first aid to the prisoner," Cherry said formally, "in order to carry out our mission and bring him back to face charges."

"Arrest him, too," Beckett snapped. He saw that some of the marines were hesitating. "Arrest him or you're all on a charge of mutiny!"

Then, quite unexpectedly, all the lights went out.

Down below

The control room door burst open and more bodies came crowding in, shouting in the darkness. It was pitch black, even with the door open—they'd killed the lights in the corridor too—so Annalie could hear and feel rather than see that the room was suddenly full of fighting bodies.

She heard a voice somewhere near her ear, and a hand landed on her arm. "Annalie? Is that you?"

"Yes! Cherry?"

"I'm getting you out of those cuffs. You've got to get your father out of here."

Her cuffs fell to the ground. She was free.

Lights began to appear in the darkness: flashlight beams illuminated marines fighting with Sundians. Essie scurried over to them. "Let's go!" she squeaked.

Cherry hurried to undo her handcuffs, then Sola's, and finally Spinner's.

"We need to get him to sick bay," Sola said.

Essie grabbed a wheelie office chair and scooted it over to him. "Get him onto this."

They bundled the groaning Spinner onto the office chair.

Annalie turned to Cherry. "Thank you for rescuing me," she said. "Again. Why did you stick your neck out like that?"

"This is not the Admiralty I signed up for," Cherry said. "Go, quick, before the lights come back on."

Annalie gave him a quick hug, then she, Essie and Sola pushed the office chair around the edges of the room, avoiding the still-fighting marines and Sundians, and escaped into the darkness of the corridor.

Essie switched on the flashlight on her shell and illuminated some familiar faces as Will, Pod, Blossom, and Graham appeared out of the darkness. "We thought you might be in there," Will said. Then he noticed Spinner. "What happened?"

"Beckett shot him."

"We need to get him to sick bay," Sola said.

"We need to get out of here," Annalie said. "Beckett's capable of anything. We can't let Spinner fall into his hands again."

"We won't let that happen," Sola said.

"Your guys are pretty tough," Will said, "but the marines are tougher and they've got bigger guns. Annalie's right. I think we should get out of here."

Sola opened her mouth to argue, but then changed her mind. "I'll go to sick bay for some medical supplies," she said. "Meet me at the side door. I'll try and find a way out of here."

Sola ran off in one direction. Will and Pod took charge of the office chair and hurried off the other way. Once they were some distance away from the control room, they entered a new section where the lights were still on.

"How Spinner doing?" Graham rasped. He was clinging to the back of the chair as the boys pushed, looking attentively at Spinner.

"I'm all right," Spinner said, with a faint smile.

"No, he's not," Blossom said. "He's leaving a trail."

Blossom was right. They were leaving a blood trail on the floor.

"We have to do something to stop the bleeding," Essie said. "What's in all these rooms? Are they offices? See if you can find something we can use as a bandage."

They searched quickly; Essie found a towel and Pod found a shirt. Blossom found a rather fascinating glass paperweight which she slipped into her pocket, but that had nothing to do with the first-aid effort. Essie wadded up the towel and they used the shirt to bind it in place, then they continued toward the exit.

A crackling noise heralded an announcement. A Sundian voice came over the public address system. "Hey everybody, just to let you know, we've taken back the control room and everything's okay. So, um, yeah. Woohoo!"

They could hear hoots of triumph in the background as the announcement ended.

"Wow," Essie said. "They did it!"

"Maybe," Will said. "I still reckon we should get out of here. Those guys of Beckett's are pretty hardcore."

They kept going. A few minutes later, all the lights went out again.

"Uh-oh," Annalie said.

Essie switched her shell flashlight back on. "What do you think's happening?"

"My guess is the marines are fighting back," Will said.

"We definitely don't want to get caught in the middle of it," Essie said.

They hurried on toward the side door where they'd agreed to meet Sola. There was no sign of her; worse, an armed marine was standing guard, and she'd seen the beam of Essie's flashlight. "Halt! Who goes there?" she shouted.

They spun the office chair around and bolted in the opposite direction.

"Why isn't she coming after us?" Annalie panted, after they'd gone what seemed like a safe distance.

"Probably ordered to guard the door and stop anyone from escaping," Pod said.

"But she's probably reported that she's seen us," Will said. "They may be coming for us."

"We need to find another way out," Annalie said.

"We should look for Sola," Essie said. "She knows all the ins and outs of this place."

"I know where we can hide," Blossom said. "Down below. They'll never find us down there."

Will shrugged. "It's better than wandering around up here. Let's go."

They found a lift and went down once more into the depths of the Ark. The doors slid open onto darkness, but as they stepped out, there was a soft click, and the lights came on.

They advanced, still pushing Spinner on the office chair, and began to walk down one of the aisles filled with old-fashioned wooden drawers. As they walked, the lights switched on ahead of them and switched off again behind them, so they moved in their own little pool of illumination in the subterranean gloom.

"We should look for a place to hide," Will said. "Are any of those drawers big enough for us to climb into?"

They were just looking around for some nice big cupboards when they heard a distant sound. Pod was the first to identify it. "The lifts are moving."

"What are we going to do?" Essie squeaked. "They'll see us!"

"Don't do anything," Blossom said. "Just stay absolutely still."

Will realized what she was saying. "If we stay still, they switch off. *Don't. Move.*"

They froze on the spot, listening in an agony of suspense to the sound of the lift descending. How long was the timer? The light blazed down upon them. Anyone who stepped out of the lift now would see them in an instant.

The lift mechanism stopped. The door went ping.

And just as they heard the clunk of the lift doors starting to open, the lights over their heads went out and they were plunged into darkness.

The only light now came from the lift area. They heard stealthy footsteps as marines deployed from the lift and fanned out into the archive, each one moving in his own little pool of light. By chance, none of the marines had chosen the aisle they were standing in; they remained as still as they possibly could, hoping that the marines would simply miss them.

They waited. Pod's arm began to itch, the urge to scratch agonizing. One pool of light drew closer and closer; they held their breath as the marine passed by so close they could hear him, just on the other side of the bank of cabinetry.

The marine passed on by and it seemed that they were safe, but then they heard something rustle and fall.

The lights above them snapped on in a sudden, blinding dazzle. Spinner had fainted and fallen off the chair.

"There!" shouted a voice.

Feet started running toward them.

Frantically, Pod and Will bundled Spinner back onto the office chair, and they all began pushing him along the aisle as fast as they could. The office chair's small wheels were not built for speed, and the chair threatened to trip them up. The marines were pounding toward them down the long aisles.

"Where can we go?" Pod cried.

"Back to the lifts?" Essie suggested.

"We'll never make it," Annalie said.

"This way!" said Blossom.

She ran full tilt down the aisle until she reached the far wall of the chamber, which was made of rough concrete. She glanced up and down it, then turned left and kept running, skidding to a halt beside a small metal hatch. "Here," she said.

It was an emergency exit.

"Where does it lead?" Will asked.

"It's an exit," Annalie said. "It leads out." She yanked it open, and they squeezed through the small door and into the tighter concrete corridor. Steps went up. They were going to have to do without the office chair.

They closed the door, but it had no lock.

"How are we going to stop the marines from following us?" Essie asked.

"Wedge the chair under the door handle," Pod suggested.

"The handle's too high," Will said.

"Let's try this," Pod said. "Lean against the door in case they try to come in."

The girls leaned against the door while Pod fought to extract a long strip of metal that held the chair's back support to the seat.

The handle turned. The girls pushed back. "We can't hold it!" Essie cried.

Will threw his weight against the door while Pod struggled to free the piece of metal. The marines pushed from the other side.

"Hurry!" Will shouted.

Pod got the metal loose and shoved it into the gap, slamming it in as hard as he could to wedge the door shut.

"That's the best I can do," he gasped. "Let's go!"

Pod, Will, Annalie, and Essie each took a hold

of Spinner and started to struggle up the concrete stairs with him, Blossom and Graham racing ahead. It was hard going and they could hear the marines slamming into the door down below. They were a long way underground; the ascent seemed endless, up flight after flight of stairs. Spinner was not a big man, but he was not easy to carry, especially in a confined space.

At last they heard a distant crash from below as the door gave way and slammed open. "They're through," Essie said.

"Hurry," Will said, although none of them could really go any faster than they already were.

And then all of a sudden, they ran into something. It was another door. Pod pushed it open and they burst out into the biting cold of the desert night, looking around to get their bearings.

"We've got to keep going," Will said.

"But where?" asked Pod.

They looked for a place to hide, but the desert was open and empty. The concrete curves of the Ark rose up several hundred yards away.

"Back to the Ark?" Annalie suggested.

"They'll catch us," Will said.

"Sola was going to get help. We need to find her," Annalie said.

Spinner spoke. He was conscious again. "You need to leave me here and save yourselves," he said. His breathing sounded labored.

Graham let out a shriek of protest.

"You're kidding, right?" Will said. "We didn't come all this way to leave you in the stupid desert at the last minute." He looked around, and his sharp eyes discovered some interesting shapes in the shadow of the Ark that had not been there earlier. "What are those things?"

They helped Spinner up, his arms slung across Will's and Pod's shoulders, and staggered on across the sand.

As they got closer to the clustered shapes, Will realized what they were. "They're all-terrain vehicles," he said. "This must be how the marines got here—they landed these off the ship and drove here. You reckon they left the keys in them?"

"No," Annalie said. "I don't."

"It's worth a look, right?"

"Are you joking?"

"Have you got a better idea?"

Will clambered into the driver's seat. "Now, how do you suppose you start this thing?"

"Let me," Spinner wheezed.

Pod helped him into the front seat beside Will. Spinner reached under the console, fiddled about a bit, and suddenly the engine started with a smooth click.

"Okay, everybody!" Will said. "Get in!"

"You don't know how to drive!" Annalie said.

"How hard can it be?" Will said.

They all squeezed in, and as the last door slammed shut, Will set the vehicle in motion. It jerked, surged, roared, paused, then began to move.

"Cool!" Will hooted. "Let's see what this thing can do!"

He turned the vehicle around and started following

the trail the marines had made on their way in, hiding their tire tracks in the old ones.

"Can you see anyone coming after us?" he asked.

"Not yet," Essie reported, watching out the back.

Beyond the Ark, the dunes began to rise and fall. The little vehicle churned through the sand, going as fast as Will could make it go.

"Do you think Sola's going to be okay?" Annalie asked. She felt bad about leaving her behind.

"The Sundians'll look after her," Will said. "She's one of them."

"That was undoubtedly an illegal operation," Spinner said, with effort. "Beckett and his men would have been hoping to get in, grab us all, and get out before the Sundians realized they were there. Now the alarm's been raised, they won't want to stick around. If I know Sola, she's lying low until they're gone."

Annalie hoped he was right.

"Spinner stop talking," Graham rasped. "Spinner rest."

"How are you feeling, Spinner?" Essie asked.

"I've felt better."

"Spinner need doctor," Graham said.

"No time for that," he said. "Just get me to the *Sunfish* and I'll be fine."

Annalie and Essie gave each other worried looks, but said nothing.

Pod was looking out the back window. He saw another shape come surging over the dunes. "They're coming!" he warned.

"How many?" asked Will.

Pod waited for a moment, but no other vehicles followed. "I think it's just one."

"You think we can outrun them?" asked Annalie.

"We can try," said Will.

He floored the accelerator, but the vehicle was already going as fast as it could. They roared up dunes, sometimes sailing right off the crests.

"If we crash, they'll definitely catch us," Annalie warned him.

"Did we lose them yet?" Will asked.

"Nope," said Pod.

The desert was very dark. The moon was not yet up and neither of the vehicles had their lights on. Nevertheless, they could see that the other vehicle was beginning to catch up with them.

"How are they going faster than us?" Will said in frustration. "There's got to be a way to make this thing go faster. Spinner, how can I make it go faster?"

Spinner peeled an eye open. "This is all she's got," he said.

"Will," Annalie said suddenly. "Remember the canyon?"

"How could I forget?" Will said, but even as he was speaking, he realized what she was suggesting. "Are we heading in the right direction?"

Annalie checked the compass and made a slight correction to their heading.

"I hope this works," Will said. "Tell me when you see it."

Will kept driving, the other vehicle in hard pursuit, the gap between them gradually closing.

"There!" Annalie shouted.

In the darkness the canyon was not easy to see—a patch of deeper black among the shadows. Will drove straight at it, never slackening his pace.

"Will, slow down," Annalie said.

"You won't have time to stop," Essie said.

"I know what I'm doing," Will said, gripping the steering wheel.

"They're still coming," Pod said, looking out the back window.

"Good," Will said. "You might want to hang on."

He drove straight at the canyon with heart-stopping speed. At the last possible moment, he spun the wheel and skidded to a halt at the very edge.

The pursuit vehicle had no time to react. Even as it started screaming into the turn, its back wheels slid out and the vehicle skidded over the edge.

Essie turned to look back, fearing for the fate of the marines in the vehicle. Pod guessed what she was thinking. "These things are pretty sturdy," he said, patting the chassis of the vehicle. "And they're wearing body armor."

Will was already accelerating away from the scene. "More importantly, they're not chasing us," he said.

He followed the canyon until the desert floor closed upon itself once more. Then they resumed their course for the coast. After a while, the moon appeared.

"Still no sign of them?" Will asked.

"No," Pod said. "But we're leaving tracks in the sand. If they do come after us, it won't be hard to find us."

Will's mouth set into a hard line. He drove on, never slowing down.

At last, they reached the coast. Annalie studied the map and the coastline carefully and then directed them north to Kinle Bay. They drove for a while through sparse coastal scrub; then the trees began to grow more thickly. When they began to see large pieces of stone, they knew they'd reached their destination.

"I hope the dog catchers have been through already," Will said, slowing to a crawl as he tried to drive into the ruined city. It quickly became clear they could not drive any further. He let the vehicle roll to a stop. "I think from here we're walking."

They stepped warily out of the vehicle. They had driven through the night; there was the very first hint of morning light turning the sky gray. Will and Pod slung Spinner's arms over their shoulders and then, walking close together in a pack, they picked their way through the trees and ruins to the bay. They were alert for the slightest snap or crackle in the pre-dawn stillness, but the only sound that disturbed them was the stirring of sleepy birds. The wild dogs had vanished.

It was a relief to arrive in the cool open space of the temple, to look out over the calm waters of the bay and see the *Sunfish* riding tranquilly at anchor, just as they'd left it. Their dinghy, too, was still pulled up safely on the rocks above the high-tide line.

"Sola said she was sending someone who knew how to deal with the whale," Annalie said. "But they're not here."

"I wish she'd just told *us* what to do," Will said.

"Whales don't like loud noises, right?" Essie said. "Could we make some really loud noise to scare it away?"

"Seems a bit hostile," Annalie said.

"Not as hostile as that whale," Will said.

"Hello, there!"

They all jumped. A Sundian man, vast and smiling, wearing shorts and a floppy hat, was walking toward them across the colonnade, carrying a bucket.

"You Sola's friends?" he asked.

"That's right," Annalie said.

"I'm Arlo. Sola's cousin." Arlo looked at Spinner and frowned. "You look a bit crook."

"I am a bit crook," Spinner said. "Be better when I get back to my boat."

"You sure about that?" Arlo asked, his brow creasing.

"Yes," Spinner said.

Arlo turned to the children. "I hear you met the temple spirit," he said, grinning.

"A spirit with really big teeth," Will said.

"She doesn't like people coming to her temple without asking. But she's really very nice once you get to know her. So, you ready to head off then?"

"Yep," Will said.

Arlo nodded. He walked down the rocks and waded out until he was knee deep. Then he made a whistling, crooning sort of sound and waited. A minute passed. Then a fin broke the surface. The huge black-and-white shadow whale cruised up to Arlo and, to their surprise, put its snout up to be patted. Arlo crooned and clucked and clicked at the whale, and the whale made noises back, then Arlo reached into his bucket and gave the whale some fish. The whale snapped them up happily, then turned and slid below the surface of the water and disappeared.

Arlo splashed back up to where they were waiting. "She won't give you any trouble now," he said.

"Was that a lady whale?" Will said.

"Temple spirits always are," Arlo said, waving a thumb at the great statue behind him.

"How do you know she won't chase us again?" Annalie asked.

"I asked her not to," Arlo said.

"Do you speak whale?" asked Essie.

"She speak human?" Graham rasped.

Arlo looked at Graham with surprise, then smiled. "We have an understanding," he said. "Anyway, you're leaving. She doesn't mind people leaving. It's people arriving that get her back up."

They thanked Arlo for his trouble and began to get ready to go back to the *Sunfish*.

"I almost forgot," he said. "You might need these."

He handed over a first aid kit and a piece of folded cloth. Annalie took the kit and unfolded the cloth. It was the Sundian ensign.

"Better fly that on your boat until you reach international waters," he said. "It won't fool anyone up close, but from a distance, you should get away with it."

"Has there been any news from the Ark?" Spinner asked. "Have you spoken to Sola? Is she all right?"

"She's fine. They're all fine," Arlo said, "although they had to do some hard fighting to take the place back."

"So they did get it back?" Annalie said, relieved.

"Yes," Arlo said. "Took a few prisoners, too. But most of those Admiralty ratbags got away. So you might want to watch out for them."

"Sola said someone was coming to help us avoid the naval patrols," Annalie suggested.

"Yeah, no," Arlo said, shaking his head. "Don't think that's happening. Now the Admiralty have invaded, all bets are off. You'd better just get out of here as quick as you can."

They thanked Arlo again and launched the dinghy with a renewed sense of urgency. He stood on the rocks and waved them off; by the time they reached the *Sunfish*, he'd gone.

They had to almost carry Spinner up the ladder and onto the deck; his strength was almost spent. But he still had the energy to notice the missing chunk of railing and deck that had been ripped away by the Admiralty's grappling hook. "What have you been doing to the old girl?" he said.

"Blame Beckett for that," Annalie said.

Spinner looked around with obvious pleasure. "I thought I'd never see her again," he said softly. "She's a good old boat." Then his knees buckled and he slumped against Annalie's shoulder.

"Let's get him below," Essie said.

Fire!

Essie and Annalie settled Spinner in his old bed in the boys' cabin. Essie cleaned the wound and dressed it using the first aid supplies Arlo had given them. They included powerful antibiotics, something their own kit still lacked.

Following Arlo's advice, they set sail due west, the Sundian flag flying from their mast. Once they were in international waters, they would turn south for their final run down the coast, and then they'd head east for Dux. What they would do once they got to Dux was another matter, but first, they had to make it out of Sundian waters without being caught by the Admiralty or the Sundian navy.

They were still in Sundian waters when the sleek shape of Beckett's ship, the *Raptor*, appeared on the horizon and swiftly began heading toward them. Essie, Pod, Graham, and Blossom joined Will and Annalie on deck.

"Is there any way we can outrun them?" Annalie said.

"We're already going as fast as we can," Will said. "And they're going at top speed."

"Perhaps we could try and lose them on shore?" Pod said.

"You mean abandon the ship?" Will said. "And then what? Go back to the desert?"

"We could try and get back to the Ark," Essie suggested.

"The Ark will be swarming with Sundian police soon," Annalie said. "If we go back, we'll be arrested."

"Maybe we can hurry them up," Will said. "Graham, fly ahead and look for some of those buoys."

As Graham took off into the sky, Will said, "If we trigger their alarm it might bring the Sundians. Right now, we could do with all the help we can get."

"I'll run up a distress signal," Annalie said, and went to fetch the right signal flag.

They kept sailing west and a little south, with the Admiralty ship bearing down from the north. After a minute or two, Graham came back and reported, "Lots of floating buoys dead ahead."

"Lots?" Will questioned.

"Two."

"What did they look like? Were they the same as the one you pooed on?"

"One same. One different."

"Spiky?" asked Will.

Graham cocked his head, thinking, then nodded.

"They're getting closer," Pod warned.

Suddenly, from across the water came a boom, then a whistling sound, and then a huge detonation blew up the surface of the ocean just ahead of them.

The *Sunfish* rocked wildly as the force of the explosion spread out through the water.

"Did they just fire at us?" Essie cried.

"Yes, they did," Will said grimly.

There was a second huge boom. This time they saw the flash as the *Raptor* fired a missile at them; it screamed across their bows and hit the water even closer. The blast nearly capsized the boat, and they all had to grab onto something to stop themselves being flung into the water. Graham flew up into the air shrieking.

"They missed!" Pod shouted.

"They're getting closer," Will said. "Those were warning shots. They're letting us know they mean business."

"Should we stop?" asked Essie.

"No," Will and Annalie said together.

They kept going, as hard as they could, but the *Raptor* kept coming, easily catching up to them, until the huge gray ship was cruising alongside, throttling back its engines to match their pace.

They heard a preliminary squawk, and then Beckett's voice came over a loudhailer. "This is your last chance," he said. "Hand Spinner over to me or face the consequences."

They looked up. Beckett was standing on the deck of his ship looking down at them, flanked by a detachment of armed marines.

"Never!" Annalie shouted back.

"You know what I'm capable of," Beckett said. "If you don't obey me, I'll destroy your boat and everyone on it."

"You wouldn't!" Essie cried.

"Where is he?" Beckett said. "I want to see him." He raised his voice. "Are you there, Spinner? Or are you going to keep hiding behind your children?"

"Your crew wouldn't fire on unarmed kids!" Annalie cried. "What about the Admiralty oath? You're sworn to defend us."

"Kids or not, you're a bunch of criminals. You've had plenty of chances to avoid your fate and you refused every one of them. So now you're going to get what's coming to you."

The marines cocked their weapons, ready to fire.

Beckett raised his voice again. "Spinner, this is your last chance! If you don't hand yourself over, you're about two minutes away from being blown to bits along with your children and all the strays they've brought with them."

"I'm not a stray!" Blossom said furiously. Reaching into her pocket, she hurled something in the direction of Beckett's head. It was the glass paperweight she'd lifted from the Ark, and if it had struck Beckett, it might have done him some damage, but the paperweight fell short and dropped harmlessly into the ocean with a plop.

"Wait!"

Spinner had appeared in the doorway from the saloon. He stepped onto the deck, pale, wobbly, but very determined. "This is between me and you, Avery. It always was. You can do what you want with me. Let the children go."

"Spinner, no!" Annalie cried.

Beckett weighed this up for a long moment. Then he smiled. "You're right. They're no use to me now. The research is gone. But at least I still have you."

"You have to promise them safe passage," Spinner said.

"'Safe passage'—what does that even mean in such dangerous waters?" Beckett said, toying with him for a moment, then: "Agreed." He turned to one of his men. "Sergeant, collect the prisoner."

"Spinner, don't go!" Will said fiercely.

"I have to," Spinner said.

"You can't!" Annalie cried.

"I have no other choice," Spinner said. "Be safe. Take care of each other. I'm so proud of you both."

Annalie threw herself at him, hugging him so tight she almost squeezed the breath out of him.

"Time to go, Spinner," Beckett drawled.

"I'm not giving up!" Will said ferociously.

As an Admiralty inflatable came toward them, Will pushed the engine as hard as it would go and the *Sunfish* leaped forward.

"This is pointless!" Beckett shouted. "You can't get away!"

"You reckon?" Will muttered.

"Will, what are you doing?" Spinner shouted.

"Trust me," Will said. "Graham, where's that spiky buoy?"

Graham, aloft, called, "Left!"

Will motored on, the *Raptor* coming up on them on one side, the inflatable swinging around to cover them on the other.

"Stand down immediately or I will open fire!" Beckett bellowed.

"Come on ... just a little bit further ..." Will muttered.

The inflatable broke off and swung away from them.

"Will, stop! I think he really means it!" Annalie cried.

"It's not worth it, Will!" Spinner said.

Essie was standing in the bow. Suddenly she shrieked, "Will! Look out! There's a mine dead ahead!"

"No kidding," Will said, still not altering his course. "Are they still coming at us?"

"I can see the guns. They're about to fire!" Pod shouted.

"Will!" Essie shouted. "You're going to hit it!"

At the last possible moment, Will turned the wheel. The *Sunfish* skimmed dangerously close to the mine, their wake setting it bobbing vigorously.

The *Raptor* was close.

They heard the order: "Fire!"

And suddenly the world erupted in a blinding, roaring flash.

The Sundians

The *Sunfish* heeled over as if it had been swatted by a giant. Everyone was thrown to the deck. Essie almost fell overboard through the gap in the deck railing. Then the shockwave rolled away, the *Sunfish* righted herself, and they began to realize that perhaps they had not been blown up after all.

"Did they hit us?" Pod cried.

Will was the first to clamber to his feet. "No," he crowed. "We hit them!"

They turned to look at the astonishing sight. Smoke was pouring from a great hole in the *Raptor*'s armor plating. Alarms and sirens were blaring and the crew was scrambling to save the ship.

"Did you just lead them into a mine?" Pod cried.

Will grinned. Pod high-fived him.

Spinner was aghast. "Don't *ever* do anything like that again," he said, white-faced.

"We should get out of here," Essie said.

"Shouldn't we stop and help?" Annalie asked, looking at the *Raptor* uncomfortably.

"Are you *kidding*?" Will said. He grabbed the wheel and set sail once again.

"Other buoy just ahead," Graham reported.

Will sailed on while the others watched the *Raptor* dropping behind. He watched the signal buoy go past with pleasure. "That's it," he called, "we're in international waters."

"And look!" Pod cried. "Here come the Sundians!"

Coming up from the south, astonishingly fast, was another vessel. It was just as big as the Admiralty ship, but it traveled under a kind of sail that was quite unlike anything Will had ever seen before. Ignoring the *Sunfish*, it was making directly for the *Raptor*.

An announcement boomed across the water. "Attention unauthorized warship. You are in Sundian waters. Stand down immediately or face the consequences."

"I don't reckon they're going anywhere," Will chortled.

He set sail for the south. They watched the Sundian ship sail past them, heading north. A Sundian coastguard officer in a dazzling white uniform looked at them through binoculars, then a voice came through a loudhailer: "All right down there?"

Will gave them a cheery wave while Annalie took down the distress signal.

"I hope they don't notice we're not Sundian," Annalie said.

"They've got bigger fish to fry," Will said. "Let's get out of here."

Will kept sailing south while the others watched the action from the stern.

"The Admiralty boat isn't going anywhere," Essie reported. "The two ships are right alongside each other

249

now. The Sundians have small boats in the water …
I think they're boarding the Admiralty ship … I'm
losing them over the horizon now."

"Let's hope the Sundians sink them," Will said
venomously.

"Not Cherry," Annalie said.

"Or the rest of the crew," Essie said.

"Okay, just Beckett then."

"Do you reckon the Sundians can take them?"
Pod asked.

The two ships had now vanished almost entirely
over the horizon.

"'Course," Will said. "Now that we've softened
them up."

The last leg

They did not see either of the two ships again. But even now, their troubles were not over.

Their course took them into the South Outer Ocean, which was known for the ferocity of its storms. A week into their journey, they were caught in a huge, horrible storm that battered and tossed the *Sunfish* for a day and a half. They battened down and prepared to ride it out, but they hadn't reckoned on the damage done by the *Raptor*'s grappling hook. It had ripped away a section of the *Sunfish*'s railing and a small portion of the deck too; Will had patched the hole in the deck, but the repair wasn't strong enough to keep out a storm. Waves pounded the boat, surging repeatedly over the deck until the patch washed away, and then they kept beating at the hole, sending water pouring in below decks, eating away at the structural integrity of the boat. They did what they could: they manned the pumps and they rode out the storm, but when it finally passed, they found that an even bigger section of the deck had broken away, and that the stormwater had worked its way into the freshwater storage tanks in the hull.

Will built a solar still and they rigged up a device for catching rainwater. The *Sunfish* sailed on. But the water kept coming in. There were leaks they couldn't find or plug. They had all the pumps going all the time, but the water would not stop. Slowly but surely, the *Sunfish* was coming apart at the seams.

They had also had no opportunity to take on extra supplies in Sundia, so their food was beginning to run low. Will, Annalie, and Essie tried to work out how many days it would take to get back, and how they could parcel the food out to make it last. Will spoke optimistically of catching some fish along the way, but he knew perfectly well they had little chance of catching anything in this vast, empty, desert ocean.

Worse still, Spinner's condition did not seem to be improving. They kept his wound clean and dressed and dosed him with antibiotics, but he seemed to get a little weaker every day. He needed proper medical care.

"But if we try and take him to a hospital in Dux, we'll get caught for sure," Annalie worried.

"We can take him to the clinic at home," Will said. "They'll look after him there, no questions asked."

Will and Annalie had grown up in a sprawling slum where there were no government services, and unofficial clinics were the only places that the slum residents, many of them undocumented or illegal, could get medical care.

"Didn't Spinner say they were still watching your house?" Essie asked.

"Yes," Will said, scowling.

"There are probably other places like that somewhere else," Annalie said. "Maybe in Southport."

"Yes, but you need to know where to go," Will said, "and we wouldn't have a clue. Go to the wrong place and it's all over."

The problem seemed unsolvable, but if they couldn't solve it, Spinner could die.

Then one morning, Spinner did not wake up. He lay in his bed unconscious, unable to be roused. Graham sat at his shoulder, nuzzling him with his beak repeatedly.

"Wake up, Spinner," he urged. "Wake up!"

But nothing could wake him.

"What do you think it means?" Annalie asked Essie fearfully.

"I don't know," Essie said. "I'm not a doctor."

But they both knew it wasn't good.

"Is there any way we can go any faster?" Annalie asked Will.

"You know there isn't," he said crossly.

They were still a week away from Dux, and that was an optimistic assessment.

Will stood for a moment gazing down at Spinner, his face creasing. "I'll see if I can do something with the engine," he said.

He stomped off onto the deck, and alternated between tinkering with the boat's engine and minutely adjusting the sails so he was certain they were getting maximum velocity from the wind.

Annalie and Essie stayed at Spinner's bedside.

"We sailed so far," Annalie said. "We went through so much. It can't end like this. It just can't." She began to cry.

Essie put her arm around her. "He's going to be okay," she said. "He'll pull through. We all will. Something will happen. Something always does."

But this time she couldn't help feeling, *Maybe, this time, something* won't *happen.*

Pod was keeping an eye on the pumps; one of them had run out of battery, and the water was visibly rising. Blossom appeared and wordlessly began bailing with a bucket while Pod fitted the new battery and got the pump going again. Soon the pump was whirring again, but Blossom kept bailing until the water was gone.

"I'm sorry about all this," Pod said quietly.

"Which part?"

"I promised I'd keep you safe."

Blossom looked at him, her bright eyes narrowing. "What? Do you think we're not going to make it back to land?"

Pod hesitated for just a moment.

Blossom, seeing it, said, "Don't be such a baby. We're not giving up and we're getting back to land. And then you're going to take me to Violeta, remember?"

"Right," Pod said. In spite of himself, her defiant attitude made him feel better.

Essie went up on deck. For the millionth time since they left Sundia, she pulled out her shell to look for a signal. For the millionth time, she didn't find any.

She thought back to the last conversation she'd had with her father. *I wonder if I told him I loved him?* She must have, but she couldn't remember, and the fact that she couldn't remember tormented her. And she hadn't sent a message to her mother in months. She'd been angry at her—was still angry at her—but now, at what felt like the last, she wished that she had.

She flicked open her shell and tried to compose a message, but words failed her. She typed and deleted and typed and deleted.

And then she heard a horn blow.

She looked up from her shell.

It was a boat.

It was large and sleek and swift, a private vessel, not a military boat. And it looked like it was coming straight toward them.

Will was suddenly there beside her. He shot a signal flare into the air; it soared up, vivid red. The boat gave two more toots on its horn as acknowledgement.

"They've seen us!" Will said. "They're coming!"

The others were all running up from below. "Who are they?" asked Annalie. "Admiralty?"

"Pirates?" asked Pod.

"I don't think they're pirates," Will said. "I don't

know who they are, or what they're doing out here in the middle of nowhere."

"Who cares?" Essie said. "So long as they can help us."

The boat was upon them in no time. It came alongside the *Sunfish*, and then a man came out on the deck, tall and lean, looking down at them with a smile. "I've been looking everywhere for you," he said.

"*Daddy!*" Essie screamed.

Rescued

Everest Wan had been searching for Essie from the minute he was released from jail. After she called him from Gantua, he'd gotten his tech experts to discover her whereabouts by tracing her shell, but by the time his agents reached the little port, she was gone. She'd surfaced again in Sundia; after that, a mix of top-level information and good guesswork had led him to the South Outer Ocean, and the *Sunfish*.

Everest took the whole crew aboard and transported them with all speed back to Dux. Spinner was put into the care of the best private doctors, just in the nick of time. If he'd gone another day or two without medical attention, he would certainly have died, but Annalie and Will were relieved to be told he would make a full recovery. The *Sunfish* too was rescued, taken under tow, and put into dry dock for repairs.

When Spinner recovered consciousness, he looked around him at the luxury of his private suite and knew at once he must be in Dux. "Where am I?" he asked, panicking. "What have you done?"

"It's okay," Annalie said soothingly. "You're safe. We're all safe."

"But—the Admiralty—"

"There's something you need to see," Will said.
Annalie passed him her shell and let him read.

ADMIRALTY "ATTACKS" SUNDIA,
SPARKS INTERNATIONAL CRISIS

An Admiralty warship was discovered in Sundian
territorial waters yesterday in what the Sundians are
calling an act of war.

The Admiralty warship *Raptor* was discovered off
the remote west coast of Sundia by the Sundian coast
guard, breaching Sundia's strict no-travel policy.

The official Sundian news agency reports that there
was an exchange of fire between the *Raptor* and the
Sundian vessel before the *Raptor* stood down and
agreed to be boarded. The crew of the *Raptor* have
been arrested, and the vessel impounded.

The Sundians are calling the presence of the
Raptor an "invasion" and "an act of war." Prominent
Sundian government figures have called for the crew
to be charged with spying and acts of war, which
carry penalties of life imprisonment and even death.

While there is no official explanation yet about
what the *Raptor* was doing in Sundia, the Admiralty
have issued this statement: "The Admiralty respects
the laws of Sundia and their right to defend their
borders. We hope to resolve this unfortunate incident
quickly and satisfactorily."

Unofficial sources say the *Raptor* may have been
carrying out covert operations in Sundia. If true, this

could make it very difficult for the Admiralty to get their crew back, as well as severely embarrassing the Admiralty on the international stage.

"ROGUE AGENT" RESPONSIBLE FOR RAPTOR INCIDENT

In sensational new evidence today, the Admiralty has revealed that the *Raptor* was ordered into Sundian waters by a rogue agent, Commander Avery Beckett.

"Commander Beckett has been a leading agent in the fight against international piracy for many years," the Admiralty said in a statement released today. "His team, which was stationed aboard the *Raptor*, was conducting a special investigation, which remains classified. Unfortunately, it appears Commander Beckett chose to ignore the very clear directives for action set down by the Admiralty and pursued his investigation in unauthorized and unacceptable ways. Commander Beckett overrode the orders of the *Raptor*'s commanding officer, Captain Gray, to avoid crossing into Sundian waters. It was Commander Beckett who forced the crew of the *Raptor* to violate Sundia's borders, and who also subsequently fired on the Sundian coastguard in an effort to escape capture. Captain Gray was then able to regain control of the ship and begin negotiations with the Sundian authorities."

JAIL FOR ROGUE AGENT

Rogue agent Commander Avery Beckett is to remain in a Sundian jail, along with four of his key officers,

but the rest of the crew of the *Raptor* are coming
home, in a deal announced this morning.

The Sundian People's Court have found
Commander Beckett guilty of a range of offenses and
sentenced him to 20 years jail.

The court accepted that the remaining crew were
acting under duress when they entered Sundian
waters, and have ordered the release of the crew and
the *Raptor*. They will be embarking on the return
journey to Dux "within the week."

Will gave Spinner an evil grin. "The Admiralty threw
Beckett to the wolves," he said.

"Twenty years in a Sundian jail," Spinner said.
"That's rough."

"He would have done worse to you," Will said.

"Don't you see what this means?" Annalie said
excitedly. "We're free!"

"The Admiralty doesn't like to leave loose ends,"
Spinner said. "In their eyes, I'm still a traitor."

Annalie and Will exchanged a look. "Actually,
Essie and her dad have been working on that."

While Everest's people had been trying to find
Essie, his energetic team of lawyers had been hard
at work looking for ways to extricate his daughter
and her friends from their complicated situation.
Their investigations into Beckett had turned up a rich
seam of potential bad news stories. Then came the
Raptor Incident. Suddenly, the lawyers had everything they needed.

Hearing that Spinner had finally regained

consciousness, Everest Wan soon arrived to share the good news with all of them: Spinner, Will and Annalie, Essie, Pod, Blossom, and Graham.

"You children are no longer kidnappers," he said. "We've spoken to the police. There were never any charges laid against Will and Annalie. The whole thing was just a fake story that Beckett's people planted in the newsfeeds."

"But the story's still out there," Annalie said. "Any time someone looks up our names, it comes up."

"We've done something about that," Everest said. He gave Essie his shell and she began to read aloud.

"KIDNAPPED" GIRL FOUND ALIVE AND WELL

Alleged kidnap victim Essie Wan has returned to her family today safe and well. She has revealed that the kidnap story was a hoax planted by notorious "rogue agent" Commander Avery Beckett, now serving a 20-year sentence in a Sundian jail.

The sensational story claimed that Miss Wan had been kidnapped from elite Admiralty school Triumph College by her schoolmate, Annalie Wallace, and her brother, Will Wallace, and held prisoner aboard the Wallace family yacht, the *Sunfish*.

The truth, Miss Wan has revealed, is far stranger. Essie Wan was forced to flee Triumph College after Annalie Wallace, Miss Wan's best friend, was targeted by Commander Beckett. He incorrectly believed Miss Wallace had information he wanted, and he threatened to harm her and her friends and family if she would not give it to him, even after she made it clear she did not have the information he sought. Believing their lives were in danger, Miss Wallace and Miss Wan fled to join Miss Wallace's brother, and the three of them escaped aboard their family's boat, the *Sunfish*. The Wallace children's father was away on business and uncontactable at this time.

Commander Beckett pursued the children around the world in an extraordinary campaign of threats and harassment which did not end until his surprise arrest by the Sundian government.

The kidnapping story was planted by Commander Beckett in an unsuccessful attempt to draw the children out of hiding.

"I was never kidnapped," Essie Wan confirmed. "Annalie and Will are my best friends in the whole world. You wouldn't believe all the brave, heroic things they've done to keep us all safe while we were trying to get away from that monster, Beckett. And now that the nightmare's over, we just want to go back to living our normal lives."

Annalie, Essie, and Will cheered and high-fived each other.

"You're so brave and heroic," Will chortled.

"No, you are," Annalie said.

"No, *you* are," Essie said, giggling.

"We've done some search optimization to make sure that this story is always the first one that comes up," Everest said. "So from now on, the links won't think that you're kidnappers. Or a kidnap victim."

"That fixes our problem," Essie said. "But what about Spinner?"

"We talked to the Admiralty," Everest said, "and they can't see the point of pursuing Beckett's personal vendettas any longer."

Spinner looked surprised. "I don't believe it," he said. "They're never going to let something like this go."

"We put it to them that since some of the research has been recovered, and the rest has been irretrievably destroyed, the object of the investigation has been satisfied and the case can be closed."

"Beckett wanted to charge us all with treason," Spinner said. "You can't just make that go away."

"You can if you properly motivate them," Everest Wan said with a smile. "Once we put it to the Admiralty that there were further embarrassing revelations which *could* be made public, about the Sundian affair and other events, they could see that it was in everyone's interest to let the whole thing go."

Annalie let out a gasp of delight, but Spinner was still resisting.

"How do I know they mean it?"

"We have a signed letter from the Director of Special Projects guaranteeing it." Everest handed the letter to Spinner. "It's top secret and confidential, of course, and there's a waiver you'll have to sign. Plus, if you ever mention this agreement publicly or discuss it in any forum, they'll deny all knowledge and the agreement will be void."

Spinner began to read it, then looked up, rather

dazed. "What about the others?" he asked. "Vesh, Sola? Dan and Sujana?"

"It applies to all of you," Everest said.

For a moment, no one said anything.

"You're free, Spinner," Will said, grabbing his arm. "You're free!"

Then they all started whooping and laughing and dancing around—Annalie and Will, Pod and Blossom, Essie and her father and Graham.

"Oh, and we're looking at getting Pod and Blossom identity papers," Everest added. "Welcome to Dux."

Pod and Blossom cried in delight and hugged each other even more fiercely.

"I can't believe it," Spinner said, dazed. "I don't know how to thank you."

"That's easy," Everest said seriously. "Never take my daughter away again."

"That wasn't his fault!" Will said, jumping to Spinner's defense.

"I made her come, nobody else did!" Annalie said at the same.

"It's all right, I'm joking," Everest said. "Mostly joking."

"He's joking," Essie said firmly. "Try and keep me away from these guys."

"Does this mean we can go home, then?" Will asked, his eyes shining.

"Yes," Spinner said, a slow smile spreading across his face. "I think it does."

Home again

As soon as Spinner was recovered from his injuries, he, Will, Annalie, Pod, Blossom, and Graham boarded the train to Port Fine. Thanks to Everest Wan, it was much nicer than the train Annalie and Essie had taken. It even had seats.

While Will, Pod, and Blossom roamed up and down the carriages and bought snacks in the dining car, Annalie sat with Spinner, watching the landscape whisk by. She had had something on her mind since that last terrifying night in the Ark, but she hadn't found the right moment to talk about it until now.

"I'm sorry about your research," she said. "I should never have brought it with us. If I had any sense, I would have hidden it somewhere Beckett couldn't find it."

"Even if you had, Beckett would have got the truth out of you somehow, and it still would have fallen into his hands," Spinner said.

"It just makes me so sad to think that all your work is gone forever," Annalie said. "When you tried so hard to keep it safe."

Spinner was silent for a moment. Then he said, "Have you heard of the Stipple-backed Bandicoot?"

"No," Annalie said.

"They're little burrowing animals that are native to Sundia. They dig huge networks of tunnels and they like living near humans, partly because we break the ground up and make it easier to dig, and partly because they like stealing our scraps and raiding our cupboards. The really interesting thing about them is they like to collect things."

"What sort of things?"

"Blue things, shiny things, metal, plastic. They take them away to decorate their nests underground."

"Okay," Annalie said, wondering what this had to do with anything.

"The Ark has quite a large population of Stipple-backed Bandicoots. They moved in while the Ark was being excavated and they've been living there ever since. The staff don't mind having them around—I think some of them quite like it, although they've had to devise systems to stop the bandicoots damaging the collections and breaking into the servers to steal the blue wires." He paused. "There *was* another copy of every piece of research. I collected a copy from each of the others and took them to the Ark. We thought hiding them in the Ark's network would keep them safe. You saw how that worked out. So it's lucky we had a back-up plan." Spinner paused. "Those memory chips have a blue casing and a little shiny metal bit in the middle of them, which makes them irresistible to bandicoots."

266

Annalie looked at Spinner disbelievingly. "You didn't ...?"

"I took the chips to different bandicoot holes and left them enticingly where they'd easily be found. The bandicoots snaffled them up immediately."

"So now where are they?" Annalie asked.

"Scattered about under the Ark in various bandicoots' hoards."

Annalie thought about this and started to laugh. "But how will you get them back?"

"It won't be easy, but it can be done. Sola has a way. Something to do with the Ark's sensors and a rare element in the chips. In the meantime, they're safely hidden away where no one will think to look."

Annalie had felt personally, troublingly responsible for the loss of the research, and it had felt like a terrible failure to have been such a central part of its capture and destruction. It was a huge relief to know that the research had not been destroyed after all. And the more she thought about it, the more she liked the idea that it had been gathered up and collected by busy little animals, living their own lives, unaware of the weightiness of the information contained inside those blue, shiny chips.

"But what if ..." she began.

"It's safe," Spinner said. "Safe among the animals. And one day, when the time is right, maybe someone will come back and get it. But it won't be Beckett."

The warehouse still stood, more or less as they'd left it, all those months before. But someone had nailed the doors shut and boarded up the windows, and a sign on the door said "Private property—keep OUT."

Spinner prised open the door and went cautiously inside. Annalie and Will, Blossom and Pod followed him. Graham flew in, shrieking with delight, and proceeded to fly around and around until he eventually landed on the workshop counter, crooning with pleasure.

"What a mess," Spinner said, looking around at the fallen shelves, the litter of nuts and bolts and broken components on the floor.

"I don't think anyone's been here since we left," Will said.

"I thought for sure someone would claim the place for themselves," Spinner said.

"Maybe someone was keeping an eye on it for you," Will said. "Somebody closed it up and put up those signs."

Pod was looking around the space with an eager look on his face. "Is this stuff all yours?" he asked.

"There used to be a lot more of it," Spinner said ruefully.

"Why do you have so much junk?" Blossom said.

Pod shot Blossom a mortified look, but Spinner just laughed. "Junk is in the eye of the beholder. Let's go out the back."

They walked through the workshop to the living quarters at the back. This too was in a state of chaos, and it looked like mice had moved in while they were away.

"Is this where we're going to live?" Blossom asked.

"Yes," Spinner said.

"Why can't we just keep on sailing?"

"Well, for one thing, I'm flat broke," Spinner said. "I need to get back to work so I can start making some money. And for another, you kids have to go to school."

Will rolled his eyes. "What could I possibly learn at school that I can't learn at sea?"

"You'd be surprised," Spinner said dryly.

"*I* want to go to school," Pod said shyly.

"Why?" Will asked.

"You know," Pod said, blushing.

"Oh yeah. The reading thing." Will was unrepentant. "You're not going to like it, you know. School sucks. 'Sit still, pay attention, do what you're told.'"

"I don't want to go to school, either," Blossom said.

"But don't you want to know how to read, and be good at things?" Pod asked.

"Don't need to read," Blossom said. "I'm already good at stuff."

"You're *all* going back to school," Spinner said firmly. "No arguments. School is not negotiable."

They all pitched in to help, setting the workshop to rights and building some new rooms on the back to accommodate Pod and Blossom. Spinner talked to Will's high school about taking Pod, and Will and Annalie's old primary school agreed to take Blossom.

That just left Annalie.

"Where do you want to go to school, Annalie?" Spinner asked.

"I don't have a choice, do I?" she asked.

"You do," Spinner said. "I've spoken to Triumph. They've already agreed to take Essie back. They'll take you, too, if you want to go."

Annalie was nonplussed, assailed by conflicting feelings. "But—but I ran away. They wouldn't want me back after that, would they?"

"They think you're one of the most capable students they've ever seen," Spinner said, "and they'd gladly have you back."

"But I've missed so much work," Annalie said.

"You've got a lot to make up," Spinner said, "but you've had more on-water experience than most of those other girls will ever dream of. They're willing to give you credit for that. The real question, though, is do you want to go?" Spinner waited, studying her. "You weren't all that happy there, were you?"

"No," Annalie confessed. "Some of the girls were pretty mean. But that's not really it." She paused. "Is it true you were in the Admiralty?"

"Yes," Spinner said. "Things were a bit different then—the Admiralty had had to get bigger very fast, and they took me on in engineering. I sailed with them for four years."

"And did you think they were good? Or bad?"

Spinner thought about this. "They were good," he said slowly. "Mostly. You have to remember, they were very bad times, and sometimes they had to do things that weren't very nice or very popular. But mostly, they were a force for good in the world."

"But what about Beckett? He went around the world acting like he could do whatever he wanted and nobody could stop him: destroying things, hurting people, and the Admiralty condoned all of it."

Spinner nodded. "I think the Admiralty chose not to know too much about what he was up to, because he was effective. Now it's blown up in their faces because he went too far, and he's ended up in a Sundian jail."

"I guess the thing I want to know is, which is the real Admiralty? Is it Beckett and the people like him? Or is it Lieutenant Cherry?"

"It's easy to think of the Admiralty as this huge, monolithic thing," Spinner said. "As if it's a giant with one point of view, doing its thing in the world. But the Admiralty is made up of people, lots and lots of people, all making their own decisions along the way. And any organization can only be as good as the people within it."

"What if the people at the top are all Becketts?"

"Well, there's one less Beckett there now, isn't there? And a few less of his protégés too." Spinner smiled. "It's easy to say that the Admiralty ought to be different. But sometimes, if you want to make something different, you have to get in there and *make* it different. Be the change that you want to see."

Annalie nodded, taking this all in. "You think I should go, don't you?"

"For all its faults, Triumph is still an excellent school. And maybe at the end of all this, you'll decide you don't want to go to university, you don't want to join the Admiralty, you don't want to be a part of any of it. That's fine, you can do that. But at least you'll have the choice."

"Are you saying I have to do it?" Annalie asked, squirming.

"We both know I can't make you do anything you don't want to do," Spinner said with a grin. "But you should think about it."

"*Seriously?*" Essie shrieked down her shell. "Of course you have to come! I won't go if you won't!"

"I don't know if I can go back to all of that," Annalie said. "The uniforms and the rules and the mean girls ..."

"Annalie," Essie said. "We faced down pirates and cannibals. We *are* the mean girls!"

Annalie began to laugh. "All right, all right! You've convinced me!"

And so, as the new term began, Annalie walked once more up the front steps of Triumph College, with Spinner on one side of her, Essie and Everest Wan on the other.

"Are you sure about this?" she whispered to Essie.

"Don't worry," Essie said. "If anybody gives us a hard time, I've got my slingshot in my pocket."

And the two girls walked, laughing, through the school doors.

Epilogue

The sky was a deep blue over the vividly green ocean.

From the top of the mast came a ripping cry: "Land!"

"What is it, Graham? Can you see it?" Pod asked.

Will, Annalie, Essie, Blossom, and Spinner each came drifting up onto the deck to see what was happening.

Pod had the binoculars out. "There's land ahead," he confirmed.

They sailed closer and closer, and the island began to take shape above the horizon, first as a dark shape. Then they began to see trees, and as they drew closer still, they saw the distinctive shape of a tower rising above it.

"The castle in the sea!" Will cried.

They all took it in turns to look through the binoculars at the island that had been Will and Essie's prison, and the strange castle-like structure that rose over it.

"It's beautiful," Annalie said.

"I think that was probably a temple," Spinner said.

"That's what *I* said," Essie said.

"Castle sounds better," Will said.

It was the start of another summer, and the *Sunfish* was loaded with all the things they'd need for a long, long summer holiday: a generator for power, hammocks to relax in, books and games and plenty of food. They anchored off the shore, and Spinner called, "Who wants to be in the first dinghy to shore?"

But Will couldn't be bothered waiting for the dinghy. He was already throwing his clothes off and diving into the water. "Last one to shore's a rotten egg!"

Annalie and Essie looked at each other, then jumped in after him.

Spinner looked at Pod and Blossom. "Come on, let's race them!" And the three of them hopped into the dinghy.

And the whole crew of the *Sunfish*, with Graham on the wing, began racing toward the shore, and journey's end.

Acknowledgments

There are many people who've helped bring this series into the world.

I'd like to thank Fiona Inglis and her staff at Curtis Brown Australia, for the support she's given me over many years.

Anna McFarlane is both my publisher and my friend and it's been fantastic to work with her again on this quest. My editors on the series, Jennifer Dougherty and Radhiah Chowdhury, have given me wonderful editorial support with the lightest of touches, and the whole team at Allen and Unwin have been very supportive of me and this book.

I was thrilled to receive the support of Garth Nix and Lian Tanner, two amazing authors whose work I hugely admire.

This book probably would not exist without the inspiration of my daughters Annabelle and Lila, whose creativity, resourcefulness, and refusal to do what they're told had some influence on the crew of the *Sunfish*.

And finally, this book most certainly would not exist without James Bradley. He is not just an exceptional writer, he is the best partner another writer could have. He keeps the whole ship afloat.

Mardi McConnochie's novels for young readers include *The Flooded Earth*, *The Castle in the Sea*, *Dangerous Games*, and *Melissa, Queen of Evil*, which won an Aurealis Award, Australia's premiere award for speculative fiction. She is also the author of four adult novels: *Coldwater*, which was shortlisted for the Commonwealth Writer's Prize First Novel Award (Pacific region), *The Snow Queen*, *Fivestar*, and *The Voyagers*. Mardi's TV scriptwriting credits include 'Home and Away,' 'McLeod's Daughters,' 'Always Greener,' and 'Pacific Drive.' She lives in Sydney, Australia, with her partner, author James Bradley, and their two daughters.